D1648875

Bilal

H.A.L. CRAIG

QUARTET BOOKS

LONDON MELBOURNE NEW YORK

First published by Quartet Books Limited 1977
A member of the Namara Group
27 Goodge Street, London W1P 1FD

ISBN 0 7043 3160 8

Text design by Mike Jarvis

The illustrations in this book are from the film,
Mohammad - Messenger of God.

The photographers on *Mohammad - Messenger of God* were
David Farrell, Mounir Maasiri, Terence Spencer.

BT
80
.P3 5C7
9pr

Printed by Anchor Press Limited, Tiptree, Essex

Bound by William Brendon Limited, Tiptree, Essex

Bilal

CONTENTS

The encouragement for a book on Bilal came from
Moustapha Akkad, the producer and director of
Mohammad – Messenger of God, when we were
working together on the script of the film. The
more Bilal entered the story of Mohammad the
more he grew in our liking.

I also thank Michael Starkey for his great
knowledge of sources and help in research.

A NOTE ON BILAL

Bilal is remembered for the love people felt for him.
He inhabits the heart. But, by the same token, Bilal was
so loved and so present in people's affections that few
felt the need to write down much about his life. It was to
them sufficient to say that he was there, always beside
the Prophet Mohammad, and loved by him. In the few
paintings of this historic moment, usually backward
glances in manuscript decorations, Bilal is always easy to
recognize. Bilal was black.

The few facts known about Bilal can be told quickly.
He was born in Mecca, the son of an Abyssinian slave
called Rabah; in a city of idol-worship, he was tortured
for his belief in one God; he was bought and freed from
slavery by Mohammad's close friend, Abu Bakr; he was
made the first muezzin, the caller to prayer in Islam; he
had the responsibility for the food supply of the first,
small armies of Islam; he was so close to the Prophet
that he had the duty of waking him in the morning.
After Mohammad's death Bilal's legs, in his grief, failed
him. He could not climb up the steps to make the call to
prayer again. He died in Syria, probably in 644,
twelve years after Mohammad's death.

Not much to base a life upon – although, from the day
of Bilal's conversion, every event in Mohammad's life
was an event in the life of Bilal. Moreover, the two
pillars of his memory, the love he had from all who knew
him and his nearness to the Prophet, are enough for a
writer who shares the first and is awed by the second.
The Black Muslims in America have renamed themselves
the Bilali. Bilal is also a patron saint, to use a Christian
description, of Moslem Africa.
Mohammad (peace be unto him) called
Bilal 'a man of Paradise'.

H.A.L.C. ROME, 1977

PART ONE

Bilal
tells of
Slavery

I, Bilal, the child of slaves, was born into slavery and continued in it until the day my owner, the merchant Umaya, decided to put me to death.

A slave has fewer accidents in his life than a free man, but when they fall, they fall. Upon him, the whip; a slave is only skin. But I am an old man now and here in Damascus I am in more danger from the thorns of the roses at my door than I am from the hand of any Umaya, or from his headaches or the caprices of his wine bottle. For a slave never knows, he only anticipates. There is no voice like the voice of your owner. You cannot hide from his voice when he calls you. If you are not in two places, under his eyes or within his shout, you have run away. He bought you and your price is the rest of your life.

It's not my habit to joke about the dead, but I can tell you that when Umaya bought me in the market in Mecca he got more than he paid for. You see, if a man buys a horse he must be careful that the horse will not one day throw him and break his neck. It happens; and when it does, the man has made a bad bargain.

But it is only God who decides who will laugh last.

I digress. I must be old indeed to digress before I begin. I cannot give Umaya, who was only a driver of slaves, too much possession of my memory. Because I, Bilal, slave of Umaya, will tell you of days to be wondered at. I was present – twenty-two years present – when Mohammad, the Messenger of God, walked the earth. I heard what he said and saw what he did.

Bilal
tells of
the man who
troubled
Mecca

That morning Umaya went as usual to sit with the other merchants beside the Kaaba.

I always looked forward to the mornings; squatting with my fellow slaves, whispering gossip, as we watched our masters, at their beck and call. But most we could enjoy the shade; and shade in Mecca is as breath to the lungs.

For nothing grows in Mecca; no tree, no grass, no flower, and the rocky hills that surround the city hold the splitting heat of the midday sun long into the night. By the rigours of nature, Mecca is among the inclement places in the world. Yet, even in those days, people who knew Mecca could never get it out of their minds. When away, they longed to return. No oasis or temperate country could satisfy them; it was always pack up and go back. Even the camels in the desert lifted their heads and lengthened their stride when the word 'Mecca' was spoken; even I, a slave, auctioned in Mecca, prodded, pinched and put to run in circles to show my stamina, grew to love the place of my torment.

I can tell you that the water in this silver cup, this cool running water of Damascus, is not to be compared to the tangy sulphurous water of the Zamzam trickling up in the courtyard of the Kaaba – though I drank it then only from the cup of my hand.

Why? Why does that brown, sun-struck city, in a desolate valley, without a single tree, without bird or butterfly, without one merciful glance from nature, why does it compel the imagination and pursue the mind? You don't have far to look. The black brilliance of the Kaaba rises up in the desert like a jewel of Heaven worn by the earth; it has shade like the shade of a thousand palms; it is the ultimate oasis. Even in pagan days it was a place of peace. No man might draw a sword or raise his hand to his enemy or bring any feud, war, disorder or brigandage to the neighbourhood of the Kaaba.

The first house of worship of the human race, the Kaaba, was built by Abraham, the father of Ismael and Isaac, who prayed to the One God only. But such was the confusion of mankind that this great house of reverence had become a warehouse for idols of carved wood and polished stone, the gods of Arabia; gods for day and night, gods for sure legs and lame legs, gods for luck and journeys. There were three hundred and sixty different gods – and all of them for profit. Not the true profit of religion, which is gained in Heaven and is forever, but the profit of the caravan, which is found in the market-place and comes and goes like spit on a hot stone.

Every year, for an agreed month, the tribes of Arabia came to visit their gods in the Kaaba. A great market grew up around the occasion and to it came merchants from Syria, sea traders from Yemen, desert carriers from Persia, slavers from everywhere. The gods and gold were equal merchandise.

I tell you all this to put my story in its place, literally where I sat in the shade of the Kaaba.

'There goes the man who talks to God.' It was Abu Jahl's voice, and his slave squatting beside me was on his feet before the remark was lost in laughter. So he eased himself down again.

'Why don't you walk on water, prophet?' This was Umaya, my master, who answers now in Hell.

Then I saw him pass, Mohammad, the son of Abdullah, walking alone as usual, his face towards the mountains where, it was whispered, an angel had talked to him. He disappeared around the side of the Kaaba, blown on by the gales at his back – or so it seemed to the laughter-makers, our masters.

But Abu Sofyan was not smiling – and in all Mecca the man to watch, after your owner, was Abu Sofyan. His story and ours are bound together as are the huntsman and the hunted, the dog and the deer. Perhaps the one needs the other; perhaps he helped make us who we are. Suddenly he stood up and the talk stopped. 'A man with one god is godless,' he said.

As usual, he had put his finger on a pulse, for pagans divide their superstitions among many gods and cannot, in their hearts, understand the pure certainty of the One God. But you could see he was worried. 'The gods will leave us and give their gifts to another city if we do not curb his blasphemy.' He looked hard at Abu Lahab. 'You are his uncle. It is the responsibility of his own family to discipline him.'

Abu Lahab was flustered. He had been sitting apart from the discussion, hoping to be left out of it. 'Discipline him? Mohammad is forty years old! I know, I know, he's becoming a disgrace . . . to me, to his own family; to you, his own class. Yesterday he adopted his slave as his son. Madness! He gives away everything he has to whoever asks. Madness! He feeds the riff-raff, the debtors . . . every day there's ten of them at his door. They're unlucky if they don't get a sheep. What can we do? My nephew is mad.'

Abu Lahab turned from one to the other as if they could help him to explain what was inexplicable – a prophet in his own country. In his worry he caught Abu Sofyan's arm.

'Tell me, Abu Sofyan: a man in his prime, strong, handsome, not a grey hair in his head, married to a rich wife, a man who can afford the best in Mecca . . . and what does he do? He sits shivering in a cave on the mountain . . . is that not mad? He has a warm bed at home! And all because of an angel he believes talks to him . . . that angel is a ringing in his own ears."

Here Abu Lahab sat down wearily. His friends were now embarrassed. A madness in the family is every man's fear because nothing can be done and no advice is right. You can only hope sanity will come back by remembering it. 'Yet a year ago, you all knew him and respected him. You wouldn't have laughed at him then. He judged your disputes and settled your quarrels. You went to him when you needed him, a man with a fair mind.'

Abu Lahab beckoned to his slave. What he had to say was said, for the time being. It is my grief that Abu Lahab at other times said more and turned towards the lime-pits when the rivers and trees of Paradise were within his reach. But only God knows the whereabouts of souls.

Abu Sofyan had made up his mind. 'What he says of the gods is one thing – serious, I agree. But the gods will look after themselves. What he says to a man is another thing – and that might be dangerous. But we'll find out soon. We'll bring in the slaves and unprotected men who listen to him.'

Bilal
defies his
master

I was standing in slave position against the wall when they brought in Ammar.

They pushed him to his knees, but he lifted his head to them. I saw then that it would end badly. Had he been a slave, he would have known the protection of the bent head. But he insisted on his rights as a free man, however low on the ladder, and dared to face them.

'What does Mohammad teach you?'

'He teaches us that all men are as equal before God as the teeth of a comb.'

I know that I, Bilal, the slave against the wall, shivered with cold when I heard these words and I know that Umaya grew red in the face and was hot. But a slave has not the same pulse as his owner.

I've often wondered why Ammar was so bold that day. He might have said: 'Mohammad teaches us to pray . . . to speak the truth . . . to desire for your neighbour what you desire for yourself,' and they would have turned him loose. But Ammar, God have mercy on him, opened the book to them: 'Mohammad teaches us to worship the One God only.'

Abu Sofyan had, I remember, a fly-swat which he would curl around his neck like a living thing. When Ammar said 'One God' the fly-swat rose like a swish of dog's hair on his back.

Abu Sofyan was not the worst – I reserve that pity for the men of Taif – and besides Abu Sofyan's own slaves thought him not a bad master. He never raised his voice when an eyebrow would do. But he frightened me with his softness and, that day, he frightened Ammar by presuming to talk equally with him.

'One God?' he asked, very logically, in a voice that seemed only curious. 'But we have three hundred and sixty gods who watch over us, who provide for us.'

I remember then something rare: a white butterfly outside the opposite window that wouldn't go away. I remember Abu Sofyan walking around Ammar. I remember. I remember. And why not? In that room, in the next minutes, all my life changed.

'Doesn't Mohammad realize that we live by giving housing to the gods. Every tribe has its worshipped god. Every year the tribes of Arabia come to Mecca to pray and to buy from us. The gods are both our worship and our revenue. And don't we look after the weak and the poor? Don't you get your share? Now . . .' he paused, as orators do to give themselves more platform, and held the room on his next word . . . 'were we to replace the three hundred gods with one, whom we cannot see, but who's supposed to be everywhere, in this garden . . . in Taif, in Medina, in Jerusalem . . . on the Moon . . . where would Mecca be then? Who would come here when they have God at home?'

Everyone seemed satisfied. The merchant prince had put down the One God and a short sentence had been roundly thrashed by a long speech. The matter might have ended there with no hurt to anyone if my master had not involved me, who had as much part in the proceedings as the wall at my back. But suddenly there was no wall at my back; my name was spoken.

In a sway of silk, Umaya approached Ammar. 'You say a slave is equal to his master . . . ?' The silk shivered on his back. 'Is black Bilal, for whom I paid money, equal to me?'

He paused to relish the absurdity of the question. I, 'black Bilal', was really outside the question, 'equal or unequal'. I was nothing and therefore neither. Indeed, I might have joined in the laughter as Umaya in a clowning gesture cupped the question in the palm of his hand under Ammar's nose. No answer was needed. But Ammar – what a fool he seemed then – dared to take up the question that everyone else, even Umaya, had dropped.

'Mohammad teaches us that all men, all races, all colours, all conditions, are equal before God.'

There was a silence. Then I heard my name again.

'Bilal.'

How was I to know that when I was called then I was called from one life to another? But it is only God who knows the next minute of any of our lives.

I came, as bidden.

'Bilal, show this man the difference between a Lord of Mecca and yourself. Lash his face to teach his mouth a lesson.' To this day I cannot understand the neatness of the phrase. Except, perhaps, that cruelty is sometimes very neat; certainly, torture is precise.

They put a whip into my hand and Ammar looked up at me, offering his face for the punishment.

How can I tell you what happened next? Even now, I cannot look back on that moment without a ringing in my ears and a sense of daze.

I remember, I suppose, very little. Umaya's bulging eyes and Abu Sofyan's profile, for he was a man who approved punishments but would not lower his dignity to watch them.

But Ammar I saw clear. His gaze was pure and peaceful, unafraid, meek but strong. I saw in his eyes a strength more powerful than my slavery. In that moment I, Bilal, changed ownership.

I dropped the whip.

I heard their gasps. They knew what they had seen and I knew what I had done. A slave had revolted.

Ammar scrambled on the floor for the whip. He tried to put it back into my hand. His whispering was like a screaming in my head.

'Do what they say, Bilal . . . here's the whip . . . do it . . . they will kill you, Bilal.'

But this time when I threw the whip down everything became calm to me. I saw Abu Sofyan gesture to Umaya. I heard Hind's light laugh and turned towards her. I had watched Hind all my life without ever daring to look at her directly. So I saw her only in flashes. I did not know, until that moment, that I had already seen all of her. She was only her flashes.

Umaya was calm, even quiet. 'If you're human enough to have gods, Bilal, then they're the gods of your owner. Mine. You will not bring any unseen gods into my slave quarters.' He glanced out at the declining day. 'I will correct you . . . but I will wait for the heat of the sun; it has passed its peak today.'

I felt the ropes on my wrists and around my neck as they did what they liked with me. I was never more obedient. Then they led me out and threw me down in the slave quarters to wait for the morning.

Bilal waits for his death

They left me alone to myself, to stir all night in myself. My master was, as I've said, precise in his punishments. A whip in the morning is the best firewood to keep a slave on the boil all night – in his description. But I had more to ponder than the whip. I had the sun; Umaya had condemned me to the sun; in Mecca, the sun was the cart of execution.

An expectation of death can light many lanterns in a man and, to my grace and favour, that night God granted me light to see by. I saw again my father and my mother working in the steam of the dye vats and the tanners' yards – my father's great strength so exploited and worn down that what should have been his full manhood was his old age – my mother coughing, always coughing, until life itself was coughed away. Yet that night I saw again their tenderness and sadness when they looked at me.

They were Ethiopians from across the Red Sea. I never knew how they came into slavery. They never told me. They endured by forgetting, although my mother said once that though I was born to slavery, I was conceived in freedom. So I always knew that in the most mysterious part of my life, its conception, I had not been a slave. Yet all men receive their life and station without their knowledge; no man may choose his door; no man may say 'I enter here.' Such is the human lot.

That night, again, in the ear of long ago I heard my father and mother whispering whether they should kill me and save me the slavery my birth had bestowed upon me. I felt again the tears on my face, not for myself, but for the pain of their love. As with Isaac, I would have submitted to my father's will and, as with Isaac, it was not to be.

I saw the day when I came of age to be marketed, to become a slave in my own stature. Then sold and re-sold among the camels and sheep of one inheritance or another, one shift of ownership to another. Bah! I can laugh at it now – from sticks to kicks to whips. But that night in

Umaya's slave quarters, tied up from the knees to the neck? I had little laughter in me.

Then, again, in streaks of pain, I began to relive the beauty of the world. The beauty that was passing from me. What was it? A dog barking in the distance; the moonlight on the floor; a man snoring across the courtyard in the depth of his peace. I hardly remember. How can I? Thirty years have gone. The mind is too limited to possess itself. Yet I do remember, in that dark night, seeing in blinding daylight a red ladybird upon a stalk. Even today when I see a ladybird I am happy all day. Ladybirds, ladybirds – what do men think about as death collects their wits?

Then there were the accidents of the evening before. What brought me to this precipice? Ammar? What had I to do with Ammar or Ammar to do with me? He wouldn't have blamed me had I struck him. He even put the whip back into my hand. Yet I, Bilal, a man of nothing, discovered that nothing in my slavery could make me obey.

You might think I made a decision. You would be wrong. For how can a slave decide? He who has no option cannot have a decision. Why then had the whip – or was it a stick – fallen out of my hands? A slave is a fear even to himself and I was neither brave enough nor fool enough to revolt. The answer lay elsewhere. Where? In Mohammad?

I had seen Mohammad many times but I had never spoken to him. When the great Fair was over, when the caravans had disappeared into their own dust, Mecca shrank. The streets emptied into familiar faces, though they passed me, the slave, without much notice and no familiarity. But Mohammad was different. He never passed any man without a look of friendship. Now he was the one witnessing the One God.

I had been lying there some hours with the ropes cutting me and my situation pounding within me. I had some hope, I suppose, that by whimpering and crawling and licking foot in the morning I might be given the benefit of the inch between life and death. I must have had hope. Hope is the last friend of a man and leaves him only with his last breath.

Morning was coming up. A new air pushed through the old air of yesterday. I filled my lungs with it. My mind began to wander back to the One God. You must know that in those days I was illiterate, my thought had no alphabet, and when I say I wandered I mean I was a nomad who possessed no wells. But I had my thirst: my thirst was all and my thirst compelled me towards I knew not what.

O God, it is not man who chooses You, but You who choose man. No man may believe except by Your will.

That dawn, by the will of God, I made my surrender to God. My Islam.

Suddenly, so great a sweetness flowed through me that I was content even in the ropes. My soul sang. I knew that my only comfort would be to be near the One God. I knew it in a truth deeper than in the mind, in the fathoms of a man, in his heart. I began to pray, and my soul rested. I began to praise God, and my mind was at peace. I began to look at His mercy, and my fear departed from me.

Then the sun rose up by God's hand.

When they came for me I thanked them. How could they have known? The proper course would have been to pray to their pity. They thought me mad. How could they have known that I had rested in the God who created me – and what they did or did not do to me would be done or not be done by the will of God? Their hands lifted me up.

How could they have known that God had already lifted me up beyond fear of their hands?

Bilal
dies and
lives

They were quick with me. They hurried me through the streets, and here and there a window closed. For people are not brutal and those who like to look at pain are few and far between. They all, of course, understood and approved my correction – I had defied, discountenanced my owner in the presence of his class. The liberty could not be tolerated. But I still had to be hurried past their houses.

To Umaya, who had a hard tooth for a coin, my case was simple. To him I was a thief. I had destroyed my value as a slave, therefore I had stolen from him the price he had paid for me. Only my hide was useful to him now; he could flay it and exhibit it as a caution to slaves. Fifty years later, I'm inclined to pity Umaya. A man who is unjust to others is unjust to himself.

They staked me out on the ground, the poor forked animal called man, and Umaya took the whip.

I will not dwell on my torture. Pain has no memory; it exists in its own present. Besides, too much has been said about that day and I have found myself too much of a martyr. But God is stronger than the sun and the soul of man cannot be touched by a whip.

I remember calling aloud to God in the only way I knew, saying the only name for Him that I knew: 'One God.' I, Bilal, who have since summoned tens of thousands to prayer, at that time knew no prayer. Yet when I spoke His name, He answered me in my heart. I did not scream under the whip, I held my breath for my God. I did not ask their mercy, but only His.

Every torture has its interludes, a recognition of limits. Had I died too soon in the shocks I would have been, to Umaya, twice a thief. It was during one of those interludes that Hind, the wife of Abu Sofyan, appeared over me in a drift of perfume and passing shade of parasol.

She leaned down to hear my words: 'One God.' Then she turned away and laughed. Hind had a very pretty laugh. 'You could swear the slave was preaching,' she said. Then the whip lashed down on me again, again and again.

I've often wondered if, for a moment, as in the swing of a tree in the wind, I went over into death. But who can tell? It is only the dead who know that they have died. Yet I can tell you that I ceased to suffer. My torturers became distant to me; even when they put the rocks down on me, weights that would eventually press me to death, I could only feel that they were doing something new and different. I was out of their reach. I watched them, engaged in their absurdities, like the dancing goats at the great Fair of Ukaz.

Then I closed my eyes and looked up to Heaven. Suddenly I saw before me green fields and trees with fruits. I heard the running of streams. I tasted the sweetness of the shade. I entered a garden where youths of every race, both male and female, walked in dignity. They greeted me and led me to a fountain. As I drank, my soul ceased to thirst and I knew I was near God.

Was it a dream, a delirium, a fantasy? Or a lucidity? Or had they crazed me with their whip? Or was it all these and poetry besides, for it is by poetry that men persuade themselves.

It was over soon, but I still ask myself: did I, Bilal, a slave under correction, see before me the land of the blessed dead?

Bilal
is bought
again

I heard voices in argument, Umaya's voice and a milder voice I did not know. I tried to open my eyes but the sun, now at its height, blinded me. They were talking about money, which was not unusual. In Mecca money was an addiction, as if men's bowels moved by money and time was told in dirham. I had no interest. I longed to sleep again, never to wake in slavery; never to be under their faces; never to be within distance of their call. For I knew now what I had never known. Even in the worst death that a man can devise for his fellow man, God is kind. In the taking of souls God's hand is ever kind.

I heard a third voice. Abu Sofyan, authority itself, was speaking: 'It is against social order to buy or sell a slave during his correction.' I tried to collect my wits. Umaya was answering back: 'The slave is dead already! If Abu Bakr wants to buy a carcass for a hundred dirham that's my windfall.'

A new name had been spoken: Abu Bakr? Why was he here? Even against the sun, I opened my eyes. There was a gasp and a stop in their talk. A moment passed. Then the voice I did not know came closer and called my name to me across the burning distance between us.

Umaya was beside himself. 'The slave kicked. I saw him kick.' Then he whispered into my head: 'Breathe, you black animal.'

It was a turnabout, to say the least. The man who had been knocking the breath out of me for several hours was now exhorting me to hold on to my last gasp. Surely, life has more comedy than it has laughter.

More voices. Umaya again. 'He's kicked his price up, Abu Bakr. He's worth two; give me two hundred and take him.'

They lifted the rocks from me and untied me. Bilal was sold again. Yes. And Bilal was bought again – but only for a minute. A young man helped me up. I had difficulty seeing him at first. Then I knew who he was. He was Saeed, the adopted son of Mohammad. I said nothing. I had no need, for he had said all: 'You are freed from slavery, Bilal.'

Umaya was counting and chuckling. 'You paid two hundred dirham for him but let me tell you I'd have sold him for one hundred.' There was laughter.

Then I saw Abu Bakr, a man like a lamp. 'You have cheated yourself, Umaya,' he said. 'Had you asked a thousand dirham for him I would have paid it.' Surely my price had shot up! Abu Bakr took me by one arm, Saeed by the other and together they half dragged, half walked me away. I was not much help to them for my legs would not hold me.

For five days I lay in a darkened room in Abu Bakr's house, drifting in and out of consciousness. Vague whispering shapes hovered over me with oils, ointments and cooling cloths. Once, when I woke, I saw a man praying in a corner of the room, but then I slept again. On the sixth morning I was able to get up and take my first steps out into the air. Abu Bakr was so pleased he brought in a goat and milked it for me. Then he told me: 'The Messenger of God himself prayed beside you for three days until the fever dropped. Only when you were safe would he leave you. I never saw a man so happy. "Bilal is received into Islam," he said. Tomorrow you and I will go to the Prophet together.'

They say I was the third man to believe in Islam. But it is too great a place they give me. I was only the ninth. I take pride in the fact that I was the lowest of the first Companions, for surely I was found under a stone.

Bilal
meets
Mohammad

His forehead was noble, prominent, and bespoke a generous mind. His smile put joy into you. His eyes, black with a touch of brown, were well opened. His hand, on greeting, was strong. His step was as light as if he were treading on water. When he turned to look at you, he turned with his whole body. He was Mohammad, the Messenger of God.

When I first came in to him, he was sitting on a simple straw mat with Ali, his nephew. He looked at me and his eyes filled with tears. Ali, who was only a boy then, took his hand. 'Why are you crying, Uncle?' he asked. 'Is he a bad man?' 'No, no,' replied Mohammad, 'this man has pleased Heaven.'

Then he got up quickly and embraced me. 'It will always be told of you, Bilal, that you were the first to suffer persecution for Islam.' Not since my father and mother died had I felt the tears of another's love on my face.

I felt like one who had been lifted up safely from the bottom of a pit. Yet I cannot recall the moment the way you might expect, as one of happiness. How could it have been? Mohammad had wept for me and I had brought sorrow to the purest heart. Nor do I understand how my Christian friends can find solace in the tears of Christ, when Christ wept for them. I have my experiences and can tell them. It is no honour to be the cause of grief in a prophet. All men say because of these tears I am a richer man. It is not true.

Mohammad took my arm and brought me to sit beside him for the first time. I must have hesitated. You will understand that I had never before sat in the presence of a member of the tribe of Quraish. My station was to stand. I know I hesitated, because Mohammad made a small joke to help me: Ali, he said, would not show us his tricks while we were standing.

So I sat by him for the first time and began there my companionship. For twenty-two years, until the night he died, I sat with him, stood with him, walked and rode side by side with him. In Medina it was I who always woke him in the morning on my way to make the first call to prayer. I would knock lightly on his door and say: 'To prayer, O Apostle of God.' Yes, I was one of the Companions of the Prophet, which is a title above princes. That day, I, Bilal, sat down to rise up. Forgive my smiling, for my little joke is apt.

When Ali did his 'tricks' happiness filled the house. He bounced and bounded, juggled and somersaulted backwards into Mohammad's arms. It was indeed a sight to see a prophet catch a flying child. Mohammad always attracted children as if he had some music within himself that only they could hear. He spoke the language of every age and would joke with children using jokes the same size as their own. One day he came to prayer in the mosque with a little girl on his shoulders, perched like an angel high over everyone, irreverently pulling at his hair. He set her down only when he prayed and then he picked her up again. Her name was Umamah.

But again I digress. I must keep to the banks of my story. My mind overflows when I think of the Prophet of God. I am living out my old age in beauty, remembering what he said and what he did. And you must permit an old man some disorder in his story.

Soon the whole household was in. Khadija, the Prophet's wife, and their four daughters, Zaynab, Ruqaya, Fatima, and Umm Kulthum, sat in a small group of their own. They all looked very kindly at me and Fatima began to ask me about the mountains and trees of Abyssinia, of which, of course, I had no knowledge.

Umm Kulthum brought round a basket of dates and the Prophet chose the softest and sweetest dates for me, trying them with his fingertips as if it would be a great disgrace should I get less than the best. For himself, he took the first that his hand found.

Then Khadija poured us goat's milk, still warm from the udder. Though fifteen years older than her husband, Khadija was still a tall, handsome woman who walked with a fine carriage. They were married twenty-five years and, until she died in his fiftieth year, he took no other wife, nor did he cast an eye. Yet every heart has some sorrow that cannot easily be put off. The sorrow between Khadija and Mohammad was the death of their two male children in infancy.

Evening was settling in and long shadows fell across the floor. The air stirred and Mecca, which had held its breath since noon, began again to breathe. On such days you can almost hear the air as everyone gasps for it at the same time. Mohammad rose. 'Let us go out into the cool of the courtyard,' he said.

I tried to follow him, when suddenly the shock and crippling of the torture overtook me again and I fell back in a spasm. Abu Bakr, who was nearest, held me in his arms, while Khadija called to her daughters to bring blankets and warm oils. But Mohammad had other treatment. 'Try to stand. Let the blood run,' he said and reached down his hands. I didn't think I could straighten my legs, much less put my weight on them. But I took his hands, he lifted me, and I rose lightly. I left all my pain behind me on the ground.

You must not suppose that this was a miracle. Because it was not. Mohammad performed no miracles. He did not cure the sick or miraculously ease the hurt of the beaten slave or raise any dead; he did not walk on water or cause iron to swim, as Elisha did. When the pagans mocked him he passed them by and never once called up she-bears out of the ground, as Elijah did to tear apart the forty-two mocking children at Bethel. That evening, when he lifted me up and my pain went from me at the touch of his hand, he performed no miracle. I laugh at the word because I knew the man. He gave me strength to overcome my pain. No more. For Mohammad could find the strength in every man and show it to him, as he found pity in every man and showed it to him.

Mohammad lived within the human capacity and died the human death. Yet God gave him a gift greater than he gave to any of His Prophets, He revealed to him the Word. The Koran is a miracle for all.

As he walked out he said in a low voice, 'Bilal, in what ways do you know God?' 'I know Him in my heart,' I said. But the answer did not satisfy me. We went a few more steps and I tried again. 'I know Him but do not know Him,' I said. 'Can you by searching find out God?'

Mohammad continued a moment in silence. He seemed not to have heard my question. He stopped and then, in that wonderful motion of intimacy and concern, he turned his whole body to me. 'Yes, Bilal, by searching. By praying to Him, by praising Him and by doing good to your fellow man. But remember always it is not you who finds God; it is God who finds you.' A great serenity filled his face and his voice strengthened with assurance. 'I am the Messenger of God,' he said, 'and I know that the way to God is Islam.'

This was the second time that memorable day I had heard the word Islam without knowing the meaning of it, although each time the word meant more. He saw my ignorance and put his hands on my shoulder: 'Islam is surrender to the will of God, who is one God without partners. Islam is doing right to all men, of every race, degree and colour. All men are equal in Islam. Islam is the religion chosen by God for man.'

Mohammad dropped his hand and turned away shyly, as if he had said too much to me too soon. 'It is all from God,' he murmured, more to himself than to me. 'Now I must go in to pray.'

So ended my first meeting with Mohammad, the Messenger of God, and so began my Islam.

Bilal
and
Abu Bakr

My circumstances had surely changed. I lived in a house without slave quarters or frightened faces. Abu Bakr was more servant than master to any who came under his roof. His first work of the morning was to milk the goats – no, I do him wrong. His first work was his prayer and after that he milked the three goats. Of all the Companions of the Prophet, men educated to kindness, Abu Bakr was the gentlest and most kind. Yet, later, when the day called for bravery, Abu Bakr was always first up with the brave.

Whatever humble task had to be done about the house he would do. Even history did not change him. When he was Caliph, the successor of the Prophet, and the ruler of half the world, when his armies were overthrowing empires, you would find him . . . where? Sitting in his doorway mending his shoes. At least, that is where I found him the day I brought him the news of our great victory at the Battle of Babylon in the spring of 634. But that morning of my Islam there were not two handfuls of us and the great empire of the Persians was still sitting safely on its throne of a thousand years. I mustn't jump my story or overthrow Persia yet.

I met Abu Bakr coming in from the goats and thanked him again for buying me. But instead he began to thank me as if I had done a favour even to the money he had spent. 'Mohammad teaches us that the freeing of a slave pleases God,' he said.

He said it with embarrassment and a slight stammer – for I was the slave he had freed and he was too honest to hide from me the self-interest of his soul. But that is the crisis of charity in every religion.

'Ah, Bilal, Bilal,' he said, 'you have new work to do. Will you slave more than you ever slaved?'

What could I say? 'Yes, master,' I said.

My reply hurt him and I knew I had stepped backwards into my own darkness and out of his sight. I had reverted to slavery and given him the 'Yes, Master' of the slave's reply. To make it worse, I had hung my head.

He put down the bucket of milk and took me by the ears – yes, by the ears – and bumped his forehead against mine. 'Listen to me, Bilal. You are a free man, without masters. But you must learn to be free.'

'Yes . . . yes . . . yes,' I said, in time with the bumping.

Suddenly he laughed and let go of my ears. 'What can I teach you? Not to be startled when you're spoken to . . . to look men in the face . . . to know that your own shadow is indeed your own? Yes, these are important . . .'

He broke off. A pregnant cat was circling the milk and I had to wait until she was given her share. I was, I suppose, put out. I'd have kicked the cat away. But I had much to learn. I remember when we were marching on Mecca, ten thousand strong, Mohammad led the whole army a hundred yards off the road to avoid disturbing a bitch in labour with a litter of pups. Mohammad, the last of the Prophets, was the first to teach mankind kindness to animals. You may go to Hell for cruelty to a cat, he said, and there will be a reward for anyone who gives water to a being that has a tender heart.

But I was new to such considerations. The cat was being fed and I was not. How could an emancipated slave be expected to enjoy second place to a cat? At last, the great, good, gentle man squatting beside the cat continued the conversation from mid-sentence.

'. . . but more important, Bilal, is a future. Slaves have no future . . they are not permitted . . .' He drifted back to watch the cat lapping at the milk as if cats might have something very important to tell him about the future. I was yet to learn that every stir of life, being a creation of God, was beautiful to Abu Bakr. Those who love God find schools in a creature and in a flower.

'If I cut you a pen, will you learn to write?'

The question was too casual, almost too unasked, for me to hear it well. Yet this was the very moment that I passed out of slavery. It was what Abu Bakr gave to me, not what he gave for me, that set me free.

I learned to write. I made ink from the leaf of the indigo, soaking it from sunset to sunrise, pounding it, then drying it in the shade. I wrote on skins, on bark, on the dried shoulder bones of sheep, in mud, in ashes, on stones – whatever would take characters. I would write with my finger in the air, so I could write.

Every day Abu Bakr cut me a new pen from the thorns of the cactus that grew around the paddock. So his day now had a new beginning – his prayer, my pen, the goats.

He would stand at my shoulder watching and helping my progress. He brought me the poems of Antara and word by word, then line by line, I learned to read them aloud. Antara was the hero of the desert; he did his high deeds, fought alone against companies, performed his chivalries and sang his songs all for love of the Lady Abla. No man in the time of Antara could match either his sword or his rhymes. My wonder increased with every line for, you see, Antara was like myself the son of an Abyssinian slave woman.

Then one day Abu Bakr came home in great excitement. I was making ink and the sight of this ordinary work increased his happiness; he took my ink-stained hands and pressed them to his lips. 'Do you know what the Prophet said, what he said today . . . ?'

He took me to a bench and told me to sit down. His news needed this small ceremony. It did indeed! ' "The ink of the scholar is even more precious than the blood of the martyr." These were the Prophet's words.'

I went back to the basin and plunged my hands into the ink and the soaking leaves of indigo. For a long time I stared down at my hands, black dipped in black.

Bilal
tells
about the
early life of
Mohammad

It is now time to tell you about the early life of Mohammad, the Apostle of God, up to the time he married Khadija.

Even in His Apostle's birth, God tried him, choosing that he be born poor and an orphan. Mohammad's father, Abdulla, never held his great son. He died when Mohammad was still in the womb, leaving him a legacy of only five lean camels and a few sheep.

Mohammad was born – as tradition and the need to name a day has established – on 20 August, in the year 570 of the Christian era. No one knows for sure. But then wasn't Christ born, as it were, before himself, before his own calendar, in 4 B.C.?

They say there was a festival in Heaven the night Mohammad was born and men heard the angels singing and saw torches in the sky. They say that the Eternal Flame which had burned in Persia for a thousand years went out. They say that a dove with a jewelled beak flew down from Heaven and stroked its wings on the belly of Amina, the Prophet's mother, so that the pains of childbirth left her. They say this and that. They say a star led three kings to the crib of the infant Christ. They say there was a fourth, a queen called Befana, who lost the star in a cloud and came late. But who can tell? They say that two angels dressed in gleaming white took the heart out of Mohammad's side when he was a child of four, washed it clean of Adam's sin, and put it back, without pain. The miracle, they say, was seen by another child who was playing with the Prophet.

All this and more was said because people sometimes want more than they need. But we already have all that we need, the Holy Koran, which is a sure guide.

When he was six, Mohammad's mother died and he was left twice an orphan. His uncle Abu Talib took him in, loving him as his own, so the boy was never at a loss for a home. Abu Talib even brought him up to Syria with the caravan, schooling him in the occupations of

Mecca, trade and transportation. Those merchants of Mecca counted well, but they couldn't write or read. Mohammad was never taught.

God chose to reveal His Word to an illiterate man, as if He needed a man who had neither guile nor sin in the written word, an untempted man, who could not fall into the traps of a little knowledge. Surely I, Bilal, who have drunk ink know how badly, sometimes, ink combines with midnight oil. Did Christ read and write? I've never known. Even when he wrote with his finger on the ground, it may have been a trick to distract attention – certainly Christ did not leave one written word.

Still the stories of signs and miracles attend Mohammad's childhood. On the journey to Syria it is said that a cloud followed the caravan, giving it shade. It is said a Christian monk examined the boy and saw the seal of prophecy, a mark the size of a large coin, between his shoulder blades. Again I can only tell what I have heard, though I confess that I've heard more of these miracles in the ten years since the Prophet died than I did in all the twenty-two years I was with him in his life. Perhaps these miracles did happen. But, as the Koran tells us, it is those without knowledge who have the biggest stomach for miracles. If I live long enough I may find some pattern in miracles – perhaps what is a miracle to one is only a parable to another.

Mohammad himself told me that he had been a shepherd and had led out the sheep in the morning, foraging for the black fruit of the arak thorn on the mountainsides of Mecca. 'All the prophets,' he said, 'have been shepherds of sheep.' Certainly, it is those who were alone in their occupation who became witnesses to the throngs of men; whether in Jerusalem or Damascus. I've often wondered why the sixteen miracles of Moses did not immediately change the world, being witnessed by thousands. But God knows best. Perhaps when he gave the Koran He departed from miracles, having no more need of them.

When he was fourteen, Mohammad was called away from his sheep to become a soldier. He was present at the Battle of the Breach, a vicious one-day war, remembered for the grief of the poetry it inspired. He was too young for a sword. His duty was to run out and scoop up the spent arrows lying on the ground, then to run back with an armful to his uncle. When he had re-loaded his uncle's quiver, he would run out again, ducking between the legs of camels, horses and fighting men in search of the terrible sticks.

Mecca the trading capital of Arabia

The pagan gods were set up in daylight or housed in the windowless interior of the 'Kaaba'

A desert tribe carries its god towards the 'Kaaba'

The great fair of Mecca

A leather shop

The wrestlers

The slaver, his clerk and his merchandise

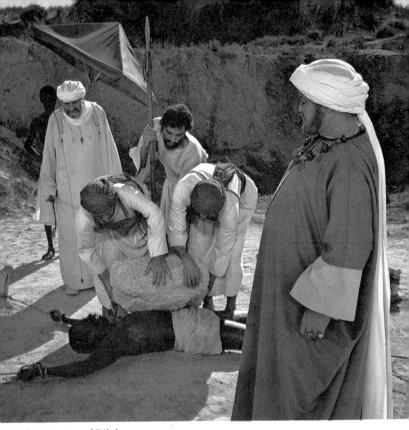

The torture of Bilal
Meccan aristocrats watch Bilal's punishment-by-pressing

The head of the great caravan from Mecca to Damascas

A halt at midday

Persecuted Moslems escape across the desert to Abyssinia

Persecuted Moslems escape across the desert to Abyssinia

Meccan horsemen pursue the Moslems

Justice at the court of Abyssinia

He never liked to remember that day, saying he wished it had never dawned. The cause of the war, a tribal dance in blood, was the slaying of a sleeping man by a drunken man. It was called the Wicked War.

If we could remove Mohammad's childhood from its signs and wonders, its following clouds and falling stars – which I am not sure we should – we might find it uneventful. In time and place, it might even be called ordinary. He began to trade in a small way, as his father had done before him, although I've never known what goods he sold – fruit or fowl, salt or pepper, scent or silk? Yet, as always, even in his ordinary occupation, Mohammad was not an ordinary man.

In a town of merchants, dealers, money-changers, short-changers and other jugglers, he was known as a man who would sell nothing on its shine. He turned the whole apple over in the buyer's hand. He could never, as the saying goes, wash a goat by moonlight.

This reputation for fair trading was so much the talk of the town that other merchants three times his age would call on him to settle their disputes. Some of his judgements would do credit to Solomon. Take that time when they were repairing the wall of the Kaaba and the day came to restore the jewel of the house, the Stone given by Gabriel to Abraham at the beginning of religion. You would think they'd have lifted it up into its niche in triumph and with joy to everyone. But that was not to be. Four factions, each wanting the honour for itself alone, stood over the Holy Stone. Blood was rising. The young men were running home for their swords. No faction would give way and none dared touch the stone without losing his hand to one of the other three.

It was then that they turned to Mohammad. His solution was simple. He swept off his cloak and laid it on the ground. He put the Black Stone in the middle of the cloak and told a man of each faction to take a corner. Together all four lifted the cloak and carried the Stone to its place in the corner of the wall. With his own hand Mohammad set the Stone.

Bilal
tells of the
marriage of
Mohammad

We can safely say – and Sura 93 of the Holy Koran supports us – Mohammad's marriage to Khadija was made in Heaven.

I first heard her name when my slave mother put a honey biscuit into my mouth. I was, I suppose, five. The biscuit had come from Khadija, she said, so the name will always be sweet to me. For Khadija was kindness. She gave, front door and back door, to whoever needed; she walked out of her way to give. She was also very rare – a rich woman who was able to imagine herself inside another woman's poverty.

At that time, before the Prophet gave women their rights, Mecca was a city of scandalous inequality. A few women were well placed and well-to-do, like Hind and Khadija, but the rest of the sex were poor and oppressed. They were men's chattels and their cisterns; by day their backs bent forward and by night their backs bent back. There had been a few poets of love, like Antara, whose verses gave women their looking-glass. But they were dead.

Indeed, it was a mystery. In Mecca, women were either prayed to or preyed upon. Three of the highest gods in the Kaaba, Al-Uzza, Manat, Al-Lat, were female. But they did as little for their own sisters as they did for my brothers.

I tell all this to show you the great gift Mohammad had in his wife. Their relationship always prospered, although it began in an unusual way. She employed her future husband as the master of her caravan trading up to Syria.

Mohammad was twenty-four years old when he led Khadija's camels north. Of course, there are the usual spate of miracles told about that journey – how he put the force of life back into two dying camels, and so on. But they overlook the greatest miracle of all, which is man and his nature.

Consider the caravan. The slow soft thud of the camels walking in the desert night, each stride a measure of journey; beast and man joined in a single purpose, the end of their travel; both tied to the same ground. But man has his head and, with his head, the heavens.

Man's upturned face to Heaven, that is the page of miracles.

Here the life of the soul begins, as the sparks fly upwards. God works in many mysterious ways but I believe He works His greatest miracles within man himself. That is why you should consider the caravan.

When he came to Damascus, Mohammad declined to join the familiar carousals of the thirsty camel drivers in the city stews. He stayed by his charges in the suburbs – knowing, I suppose, that more sailors are drowned in port than on the open sea. He served his employer with a sober head and came back to her with more than she expected. Khadija was always quick to see and when Mohammad came home from Syria she saw her husband.

She sent Nafisa, a go-between, to ask him in a roundabout way if he had any intentions of marrying. 'But I possess nothing to marry with,' Mohammad replied. Nafisa poked him in the ribs pretending that his plea of poverty was merely coy hesitation. 'But suppose there was someone who had enough for two?'

Then she leaned in close and continued in a whisper. 'Suppose you were invited to beauty, to wealth, to a position of honour, the master of a noble house . . . would you accept?'

Mohammad was wary. 'It might depend upon the woman.'

'Naturally.'

'Who might the woman be?'

'Khadija.'

Mohammad jumped up full of happiness. 'What must I do?'

Nafisa sat him down again. 'Leave everything to me.' But Mohammad was up again. 'No, no. I must go and tell her that I've admired her since I first met her, but could never dare to speak.'

A giggling Nafisa followed after a young, striding caravan master.

Khadija was then nearly forty years old and twice widowed; Mohammad was twenty-five. I've heard some cynics here in Damascus saying that he, not she, was caught. But they know nothing.

This marriage was so perfect that it might have been an angel, not a go-between, that proposed it. It was the first step up towards his mission. Khadija freed him from poverty, allowing him to undergo the hard work of the soul, the lonely agonies and contemplations, the doubts and uncertainties that were his education. She comforted him in his despair and, I heard him say once, 'when they called me a liar, she alone remained true'. She was the first to believe in his mission, before anyone, even he himself, believed in it.

Yet in the bearded opinion of Mecca their marriage had a flaw. Mohammad had no male heirs. In compensation he was awarded four girls, of whom Fatima was one. It was as if God decided for His Prophet that woman was indeed 'the proper companion of man'.

Bilal
tells of
Mohammad's
Call

What I relate now I have by authority. I was told it by Abu Bakr, who heard it from Saeed, who had it from Ali, who knew it from Khadija, who received it from the lips of Mohammad, who experienced it. Moreover, it is confirmed, in the second part, by God in eighteen verses of the Sura of *Najm* (meaning the Star). Therefore, it is a fact irrefutable and an evidence of religion.

Mohammad was alone in a cave on Mount Hera when the Angel Gabriel came in to him.

Gabriel said: 'Read.'
Mohammad replied: 'I cannot read.'
Gabriel commanded again:
'Read in the name of thy Lord,
Who created man from a sensitive drop of blood,
Who teaches man what he knows not,
Read.'
Still Mohammad replied: 'I cannot read.'

Then Gabriel wrestled with him, pressed him down and smothered him until he thought he would die. But in his last extremity Gabriel released him and left the cave. Mohammad knew that a message from God to man was written within him. But he did not yet know what.

He could not bear the load. He wanted to kill himself. He went scrambling up towards a steep place on the mountain from where he might jump off into oblivion. But halfway up Gabriel again appeared to him. Now he saw Gabriel clearly in the figure of a man standing on the horizon with crossed legs. Wherever he looked, wherever he turned his head, to north, south, east or west, at every turn he saw Gabriel.

Again he heard the voice of the Angel: 'Mohammad you are the Messenger of God and I am Gabriel.'

He ran home and hid, shivering, under blankets. Was it a vision from God or was he the fool and victim of a devil? Was his mind diseased? Had the moon struck him? Was he swept by a storm in his brain? He knew he was only a man.

He piled up more and more blankets. Then Khadija came running and he told her what had happened. He laid his head in her lap and told her everything.

Now there are those who still must deal in the marvellous and must colour each occasion. They say the Angel followed Mohammad home and stood where only he could see him. He pointed to the place, but Khadija was not permitted to see.

Then Khadija sat Mohammad on her knees, undid her clothes and exposed herself, whereupon the Angel fled. She had proved that the Spirit was good – an evil spirit would have stayed to look, whereas a good spirit must retire in shame. But pleasing stories are not always the best truth. I leave them to the smoke of the campfires.

I edge towards what I know. God had gifted Khadija with her own insight. She comforted her husband, subdued his fears, reasoned with his uncertainty. Above all, she comprehended the mystery and, while he himself was writhing in humility and self-doubt, she believed.

She fortified him. She told him that if God was God, God would not deceive a truthful man. Throughout the night she held him to what the Angel had said. 'Mohammad, you are the Messenger of God.'

They call this night Laliat Al-Qadr, the Night of Majesty. In this night God gave man his daylight. In this night God permitted Gabriel to bring down the Holy Spirit. In this night God endowed His Apostle, Mohammad, with his first knowledge. In this night, Khadija also believed and became mother of the Believers. In this night God sent His mercy to mankind.

No one knows for sure when this night is. In Ramadan, yes. Ramadan is the month of fasting, revelation and mystery. But Ramadan has thirty nights, beginning and ending with the thread of the new moon, and the Night of all Nights, the Night of Majesty, is hidden among the thirty. Some say it is the seventeenth, others the twenty-third, or the twenty-fifth, while others insist on the twenty-seventh. In the Koran it is revealed that this night is better than a thousand months – yet only God Himself knows when this night falls.

I have since climbed the mountain many times to the Prophet's cave. The mouth is so low you must stoop to go in and inside you can only crouch. Yet this is the first room of the Message, the auditorium of Heaven. Each time I go up I feel my knees begin to fail me and I have to clutch something for fear of falling. But the same happens sometimes when I see great beauty – then, too, I must hold myself up. Our best moments often disable us.

A man can see far from the top of a mountain, out over the heads of small concerns. From Hera you look beyond Mecca into the brown distance of the Hejaz, where tribes move, where caravans journey and shepherds have stood since time immemorial beside their flocks. It is a world laid out in beauty and occupation, in harshness and adaptation. Yet it moves in silence, for no discord or human voice reaches you on the top of the mountain. Your ears are open to God.

Bilal
witnesses
Revelation

You might envy us, who had the first bright happiness of Islam. But I'd also ask you to pity us. We trembled lest our minds were unfit for the knowledge; even Noah ran and hid himself from the approach of the Divine. We were limited uneducated men, none of us equipped to bring an order, much less to apply ologies or isms to the great truths we knew so clearly in our hearts. Today the young know everything – I even catch my son at angles and triangles; he holds facts by the camel-load in his small head – but all we held were the small, immense lamps of the early verses.

> Say that God is One,
> The Eternal God,
> He begot none
> Nor was He begot,
> No one is equal to Him.

Many and many a time I saw Mohammad, the Messenger of God, in the very moment a revelation came down to him. Suddenly he would start to tremble and look around for some corner or hiding place. In the coldest nights I saw the sweat run on his face. I saw the pain strike him, his body shuddering, his hands gripping his sides in the spasms. He might lie for an hour without hearing one word spoken to him – and why not? He who is called by angels is deaf to men.

He never knew when a revelation might come down. He might be in the middle of a conversation or going about the house or even riding on his camel. Then he dismounted quickly and covered himself with his cloak. Sometimes, at the beginning, he heard bells or passing wings or a sound like the clinking of chains. Often an angel appeared and spoke to him, but we who were only an arm's length away neither saw nor heard.

God's revelations to His Prophet were not in words as we use them to each other – surely God made our mouths as the very hollows of our heads! The Message was pressed down on Mohammad's heart, and only after the Prophet had got up and come back to us did God permit him to recall the inspiration in words. But not one syllable, not one noun or verb was out of its proper order. Then it was written down on skin or bark or shoulder-bone of sheep – whatever was at hand. All was as Gabriel gave it, unaltered.

When I saw his human distress, I have to admit that sometimes my awe of prophecy was overtaken by my love for the man. I wanted to go to him, but my feet stood still – for who can dare God? He told us once what he underwent in these exalted moments. 'I never receive a revelation,' he said, 'without thinking that my soul has been torn away from me.'

Revelation followed revelation, until Heaven itself seemed busy, and we lived in joy. We were young. We stood at the beginning. Every dawn rushed to our heads. But we saw no dancing sun. For the Koran is a miracle without works, a victory without processions, even a book without writers.

Bilal
tells of
the hatred of
Mecca

Why did they hate us? They were not evil men; they were out of old traditions, even out of old decencies. They followed customs of hospitality and obeyed their own rules of honour and dishonour, obligations in the give and take of a desert existence. The hardness of their hearts was mostly the result of the hardness of their lives, as those who live on the backs of donkeys are the most terrible at beating them.

They did not hate us and our One God because they loved their many gods. The love of the gods was never much in paganism. Gods were exploited and anointed at the same time. It was a system of exchange, a merchant's deal with the devil. 'I will worship you, Hubal, and do you honour and bring you a present and continue your exist-ence by coming to you – if you will help me find my lost camel.'

But I, Bilal, who once worshipped pagan gods, must not be too light with them now or I risk ignorance. I must tell you plainly about the strength and weakness of the gods.

We talk of gods of wood and stone, but no pagan was ever stupid enough to worship stone which he could crack or wood he could burn. He conceived a spirit residing in the wood or stone and worshipped that spirit. Yet here, also, was the weakness. The gods had a residence, like the Kaaba, and their divinity stopped short at the next idol, the next temple, the next tribe, the next city, the next god. The god that opened the door in Mecca couldn't even shut it in Medina. So much for the power of gods.

But worse. The gods were both above and below their worshippers. Even the Romans, in their pagan days, knew how the gods depended on man. Gods fall out of service by not being named; when they are not worshipped they cease to exist. Julius Caesar had his gods and Augustus Caesar had his; gods came and went in a change of togas. Men made or unmade their gods simply by giving them more or giving them less, bowing to them or walking past them, which was a very bad power to entrust to man.

63

Only by a blind gift from God can man remake himself.

One reason why they hated us was their incomprehension of the power of the One God. I remember how they used to fret when Mohammad preached the resurrection of the body. Once Abu Lahab, who was so fat that he had to be helped up, brought the Prophet a piece of human bone and began to crumble it between his soft fingers. 'You say this can resurrect? This can be made man again?' he asked and blew the powdered bone in the Prophet's face. Mohammad brushed off the dust and looked at the heaving, angry merchant prince. 'God who made man in the first place,' he said, 'can remake him again if He wishes.' I always feared Abu Lahab and I feared him most then. The ground around him shook with the weight of his outrage. But maybe even the devil is modest. Abu Lahab could not conceive that at least one part of his vast presence in this world, if not his importance, might be continued in another.

Yet every pagan I have ever met has suffered from too proud a logic. Unable to submit to what he cannot see, he reasons that man is all and each man is the end of himself. His afterworld is his underworld, a grave without opening. Even mighty Julius Caesar on the day of his triumph, standing at the altar, declared: 'Death is the end of everything.' It was a proud mastery of fate and a contempt equal only to the omniscience of suicide. But while man can endanger his soul, corrupt it, deform it and blacken it, he cannot kill it. There is hope only for suicide of the body, none for the soul. Each man must answer to his own indestructibility. Yet Abu Lahab thought he could disprove God by rubbing a bone between his fingers.

But to give him every credit, Abu Lahab's anger had an eye. He attempted to dispel a mystery by digging up evidence from a grave. His friends were less perceptive and our small, ragged band was a cause for their merriment and jokes and an excuse for more wine.

They mocked us, spat at us, pelted us with dung and hatred. We might wash off their spit, which was merely their slime, but the insult to the Prophet bled within us. How could he, beloved by Heaven and regarded by angels, be the laughing stock of dying men? We saw only light denied. Yet he bore all with patience and mildness. Surely patience is the equipment of a prophet, a breastplate given to him by God. I was not so equipped.

The children of Taif stoned the Prophet back into the desert

The Hegira: the flight from Mecca (Year One of the Moslem calendar)

The Hegira: the flight to Medina
(Year One of the Moslem Calendar)

The Hegira: the flight to Medina

Medina: waiting for the Prophet

Medina: the people
rush out in welcome

Quaswa the camel,
is turned loose

Quaswa, the camel,
has chosen

The Mosque at Medina

The Meccan army on the march

The Meccan army approaches Badr

Part of the Moslem army drawn up before the Prophet's tent

The Moslem army waits

The Meccan army attacks

The attack is turned back

The Meccans press the attack

The Moslems counter-attack

The surprise cavalry charge defeats the Moslems at Uhud

The Moslems thrown back against the mountain

Unarmed Moslem pilgrims approach the well of Hudeibiy

They got round me one day, Ikrima and half a dozen more, and pointed their fingers at me. No one said anything: no word, no sound, just a small smile on every face. I was frightened, I suppose. Yes, damn them, I stuttered. If I turned to my right, one of them jabbed his finger into my left side until I was spinning like a top. I couldn't hold my water. My urine ran down my leg. I was caught in their net of fingers and smiles. They knew how to point down and measure out an ex-slave.

They went away laughing.

Looking back at them now I know that they hated us for the most human of reasons. It is an unhappy law that wherever truth raises its head you will find men rushing to cut it off, as if some monster had come into their lives. Truth is always first seen as an enemy and run at with hatred and derision.

Bilal
tells
when the
laughing
stopped

Sooner or later the laughing had to stop. Abu Sofyan was not a comedian, his fly-swat rose and fell in monotonous motion, in a kind of thought. He knew from the start that Islam was revolution. Mohammad was not only preaching a new measure of God, he was also teaching a new measure of man. Islam threatened property, whether large or small, with a religious tax: those who have must share with those who have not, in money, produce and possession. Yes, this was revolution. Islam threatened the power of the merchant nobility, whether personal or political, by giving rights to the weak and by denying the exclusive birthrights of the tribe. Moslems owed themselves to God, not to their families. Arabia could not tolerate such a future.

Abu Sofyan tried, they all tried, to make Mohammad see reason, meaning, of course, their point of view. They offered him bribes of position, authority, even income from the Kaaba. They thought, poor fools, that prophecy might be bought with the minerals of the earth. But he turned the impossibility back on them. 'Were you to put the sun in my right hand and the moon in my left, I would not renounce my message, which is from God.' Then he looked at them with pity for their souls. 'Do not murder your children,' he said, and walked away.

I must explain to you what was meant by the murdering of the children, because in thirty years Mohammad has spun the world forward so fast that I wonder sometimes if we are still walking on it and not thrown out among the stars.

He meant precisely what he said. 'Do not murder your children.'

Before Islam, in the desert, a child's fate was known even before its toes were out of its mother's body. If the child was male it was safe and celebrated; if female, unsafe and whispered over. Had they a sufficiency of girls in the family or too many in the tents of the tribe, she could be doomed. When they had bitten the cord, she was taken out into the desert and the sand was shovelled over her.

They did not commit murders without niceties, and their arguments for female infanticide were, of course, logical. They were saving life by taking it; the economics of the desert, not they, decided the issue; a new mouth was another's empty belly; besides, the female will breed and multiply herself. On and on they went improving even on the selection of God. More females are born than males; they were merely correcting the imbalance. A few girls certainly were worth their puberty and they saved those for later use.

It was sad to hear them. The design of creation had no holiness for them. Yet who can cry shame upon whom? When Mohammad was preaching the equality of women in Arabia, in France a council of Christian bishops was meeting to decide if women had souls or not. I don't know how they decided – up here in Syria you're told everything and nothing. Yet I often wonder at the contradictions by which religions regard women and how the same people who venerate Mary, the mother of Christ, can so lightly desecrate Eve, the mother of man.

What most angered them, more even than the denial of the gods and the saving of the children, was the limitation of wives. Before Mohammad, a man might marry as often as his thighs desired or his camels provided. Some had ten in bed, some twenty, each one crawling over the other to get closest to her king.

Islam limited the wives to four, with a commandment that made it more comfortable to have only one. All four must be treated equally and their claims on marriage must be satisfied equally by turn. If these claims could not be satisfied, a man could take one wife only.

Did the women rush into their new dignity? No, they too scorned the Prophet. Indeed, I can still hear the civil war of the women. If the fifth wife were sent away who would pick her up, who would take her in, who embrace her, who husband her, who feed her? In the desert it was customary to have many wives, not just because men are rapacious but also because men are generous. So the limitation of the wives was a bewilderment that at first seemed an unkindness, even a cruelty, to women.

Mohammad did not stop there – how could he, with an angel upon his heart? He insisted that women, though different, were equal to men. The difference is easy to find, men are clustered and women are cleft, but to see equality in sex you had to shade your eyes. He told them that women are complementary to men, each is the guardian of the other. Both must submit to the same last judgement and both will inherit the same fate.

The world that now loves Mohammad hated him then for these simple ideas. One age mocks what the next adores, and fruit is bitter before it can be sweet. Yet give an old dog on the road the right to bark. I sometimes wonder if even God knows which of us, my wife or I, He made equal. She blew out the candle on me last night when I was in the middle of a book by Herodotus. If I didn't love my wife more than my Herodotus, I'd have hit her on the head – but maybe she was saving me from reading the heathens.

But, as I've said, the laughing now had stopped.

Bilal
tells of the
persecution
and the
flight to
Abyssinia

Old as I am, near death as I must be, I still outrage at cruelty. I damn cruelty. I who have known cruelty have, more than most, the knowledge to pray against it. Surely Heaven listens to a man who knows what his prayers mean.

I pray that the torturer be compelled to see himself in
the body he abuses. Grant him this one sight only because
he deserves no other.

I pray that the hangman be not denied his own neck or
the judge his own justice.

Let those who stand waiting before judges be the judge
of them.

Let no judge sanctify law unto himself and make it his
calf, for earthly law, like heavenly law, is in the dominion
of God and he who abuses it with cruelty abuses God's
mercy.

Let torturers be exceptional and answer twice for their
sins. I pray that they be struck for their sins, even as they
commit them.

This is the prayer of Bilal, who is black, born a slave and who damns cruelty. But I moralize. I promised you history and you shall have it like meat turning over on a spit.

Suddenly they were down on us with cruelty and murder. Not a day passed without some act of injustice against the soul of man, until Heaven itself wept in the Prophet's eyes – or so we felt, as we watched his grief. But he would not, could not, step out of his path. It seems to be God's will that the footsteps of prophecy be set painfully in solid rock, yet to those who come after the same steps seem light and happy with great and good news.

The first martyr to suffer death for Islam was a woman. She was awarded Paradise when Abu Jahl, in a fury of paganism drove his spear into her side. Her name was Somaya and she was the mother of Ammar. Her crime? She refused to pray to Hubal.

Others were staked out and flogged to death or to its door. A few gave in and foreswore Islam, it is true, but, I, who knew the lash, forgive the flesh. Perhaps God did not wish them to suffer more than they could bear and allowed them to deny Him. God is ever merciful. God never puts on a man more than a man can bear.

Mohammad had to act. They were taking us one by one. He decided that the weakest, those who had no family protection, should run from the country; the others, whom they dared not harm without risking family feuds or even tribal encounters, could stay for the time being. I, who was now protected by Abu Bakr, was chosen to stay.

One night Jaafar, Ali's older brother, with ten men and three women slipped off into the desert. Their destination was Abyssinia, my never-known country across the sea, then ruled by a Christian king famous for his quality of justice. They dared not take the usual tracks and had to push through the hardest part of the desert, without wells or people. It was said of these first refugees that their only shade was the wings of the vultures wheeling over their heads, waiting for them to die.

But there are more eyes in a small town than in a big city and the flight was soon discovered. Abu Sofyan sent out a party of horsemen to bring them back or, depending on the going, to finish them in the desert. The horsemen found their footprints and even rode beside them for a mile. But God did not permit them to see or their horses to smell. Jaafar passed unharmed through hoofs and swords, and if you want to believe a miracle, you can. I'd rather believe that Jaafar knew how to use the desert, its blinding glare and the long black shadows of the dunes. If there were miracles, they were his, for he was a man who could hide himself in his own shadow. But, without doubt, God gave Jaafar his wits.

When we saw Abu Sofyan's horsemen come dragging back to Mecca with nothing to show for their search but their sore eyes, we put our policy into escape. We began sending away others, until eighty-three of us, men and women, had crossed the Red Sea to Abyssinia.

But even in Abyssinia our people were not safe. At home Abu Sofyan's voice became softer, lower and even more dangerous. I'm told that at this time you had to lean forward to hear him. If you sat back his words dropped down in front of you and you heard nothing. But if you leaned an inch forward, you heard everything, clearly, exactly and in fine sentence. You see, his dignity was in question. Mecca could not allow eighty-three dissidents to run loose in a neighbouring country – it was bad for trade. If they failed to get them in the desert or on the sea, then they would go where they were hiding – behind the throne of the king, who called himself the Lion of Judah.

An embassy led by Amr ibn al-Ass was sent to the Lion of Judah, armed with presents, apologies and letters of friendship. Amr, who has since conquered Egypt, was then a smooth boy with everything at his fingertips. But thank God he was too clever to succeed or else he would have put eighty-three souls into chains and his own soul into hell-fire. As I will tell you, God granted Amr the mercy of failure.

The king called the Moslems before him and asked them to show cause why they should not be returned to Mecca in chains. Poor Jaafar was like Daniel in the lions' den. He stuttered, stammered, even stumbled, hardly able to put two words or his two feet together.

Amr, for his part, shone with indignation, mounting his arguments on the very back of scripture until it seemed that prophecy was the ass he rode. He accused Jaafar of sedition, of using the pretext of a false prophet to undermine the social order, of blasphemy, desertion, and finally and emphatically he proved all of Islam to be absurd. Amr was, of course, as pagan as a piece of stone but even then he knew a little about religion and a lot about mockery. In a few minutes he had the whole court of Abyssinia laughing and the chains for Jaafar clinking on the floor. But God who made the cleverness of man, also gave him his stupidity and sometimes He mixed the two in the same head. So it was with Amr, who lost when he had won – or, as surely as I sit here in history, won when he had lost.

It happened this way. Jaafar spoke of Jesus Christ as we Moslems know Christ, a prophet in the line of the prophets who came before Mohammad, who is the seal of all the prophets and the last. Yet Christ was so loved by his people that they fell into the error of worshipping him.

Even in Abyssinia, Jesus was loved to such depth that the mention of his name brought a tear to the eye of the Christian king. Amr saw the tear but mistook it for a glisten – surely blindness of the spirit is a condition so terrible that Christ himself needed a part of his own body, his spittle, to cure it. Amr at that moment was blind. He flipped his cloak and stood with both legs astride – like a headsman upon his axe, Jaafar told me – then he delivered what he thought was the finish. 'They lie about Christ,' he said. 'They say your Christ was merely another prophet and not the son of God. They say you worship three gods, one a father, one a son and one an invisible. They deny the divinity of your Christ and make him a dead man.'

How well-versed this pagan was; how well he seemed to know every religion; how subtly he put the Moslem understanding of Christ into a contradiction with the Christian understanding of their Lord. The king turned at Jaafar. 'Tell me about the mundane birth of our Lord.' He swept the word 'mundane' off with the back of his hand and motioned to the jailers to come forward. But Jaafar stepped through the jailers.

'I will tell you what the Holy Koran says about the birth of Christ, which is all I know.'

It was at best a despairing shout, but it lifted the head of the king. Jaafar then found his voice. He had to. His only hope was to speak out, speak at the chains, speak at the frown of the king, speak at the four lions that growled in heavy stone about the throne. Some say, though I apologize for the use of the name, he spoke as well as Bilal – Amr ibn al-Ass himself said it to me ten years later. But Bilal is only a trumpet, the orator of the time for prayer, who has the advantage of speaking from a height; Amr can still catch flies in his own honey.

Jaafar that day knew how to speak persuasively, like a man who has no choice. He recited to their astonished faces the verses in the Sura of Mary, Sura 19, that tell of the birth of Jesus Christ from the womb of a virgin. He placed the lines properly in their understanding, so that they knew it was God Himself who was speaking, not 'God the Father', but God.

Relate in the Book
The story of Mary.
How she withdrew
From her family
To a quiet place.

Then We sent to her
Our Angel, who appeared
In the shape of a man,
Fully grown.

When Mary saw the man
She cried out for help,
Imploring him not to molest her
If he feared God.

But Our Angel replied:
'I come from your God
To announce to you
The birth of a holy son.'

'How shall I bear a son,' she said,
'When no man has touched me,
And I am still a virgin?'

'To your God all is easy,'
Our Angel said.
'And He will appoint your son
As a sign to men
And a mercy sent from God.
It is a matter determined.'

Thereupon she conceived her son
And retired to a remote place.
In the pains of childbirth
She lay down under a palm tree
And cried out:

'Oh that I had died before now
And passed into oblivion and become
A thing forgot.'

But the voice of the Babe from below
Spoke to her.
'Do not despair. Your Lord
Has caused a brook to run
At your feet.
And if you but touch the tree
It will let fall
Ripe dates into your lap.
So eat, drink and
Rejoice.'

The whole court was moved to tears and murmurs and the Lion of Judah left his throne to embrace Jaafar. Instead of chains he now had the arms of a king about him. 'Not for a mountain of gold will I give you up to them,' he said and drew a line on the floor with his staff to show how narrow was the difference between our Koran and his Gospels. Amr stood by shuffling his feet. Then, Amr, being Amr, nodded to the king with a smile as if everything was just a gamble and the dice he threw had rolled wrongly.

That was Abyssinia, a land of lions and honey – and justice. But in Mecca, a city of caravans and rates of exchange, it was silk, spice and perfumes, not justice, that was weighed in scales. The Word was still unseen; their ears heard it but their hearts remained blind.

A new persecution, more cold blooded than the whippings, now fell upon Islam. It was nothing less than the punishment of a people. The entire Beni Hashim, the family tribe of the Prophet, was put under ban. No one could treat with them, give them shelter or hospitality, a pinch of salt or stir of sugar, not even shade could be given them. They were declared outcast and exiled to the desert, carrying only what their backs could support. Whether they believed in Mohammad's message or not, whether they listened to him or not, liked or disliked him, they were all persecuted equally with him. It was enough to be a member of his family, even the cousin of a cousin, to find oneself driven out into the open desert like a man with a disease. It was a solution worthy of its author, Abu Sofyan – send Islam out to die of itself, of its own madness, in the sun.

For three years we suffered the hunger and thirst of the desert, lying in makeshift shelters behind hedges of thorns. Children died by day in the heat and the old died by night in the cold. Everywhere we walked we had to step over misery. We looked to the sky but no manna fell to us as it had come to Moses. Still, we endured and came to realize that if cruelty does not break a man's back, it will strengthen his spine. Perhaps this was a gift more than manna.

Bilal
tells of
the conversion
of the giants

Although we did not know it, while we lay there in the desert events like clouds were gathering around us. It is true that we had yet to reach the bottom of misfortune; other blows would fall, new knocks, new calamities. But first there was a stir of hope that lifted all our heads. Hamza and Omar converted to Islam.

It is strange how both conversions began with rage and a bloody face. Hamza led the way. He was Mohammad's uncle, a huge man famous throughout the desert as a lion hunter and warrior. In battle no sword was heavier, no spear faster, no arrow deadlier than the weapons of this warrior and in the hunt no one was braver or more delicate or light of foot or sharp of eye or keen of smell than this killer of lions. Yet out of the strong comes sweetness and Hamza, huge Hamza, was a man who would wheel his horse around a desert flower rather than crush it. At times he was a roaring poet in the wild epic style, which fitted him.

But there was no sweetness in Hamza the day he rode into Mecca and heard Abu Jahal declaring that Mohammad was both a liar and a fraud. Hamza had a dead, full-toothed lion tied to the rump of his horse, but even that wasn't hint enough to Abu Jahal to mind his tongue. He repeated the slander and that was unwise. Hamza, with his hunting bow in his left hand, strode through the crowd as if no crowd was there. He said nothing, the only sound was the thump he gave Abu Jahal with the back of his bow, sending him sprawling with the blood running down his face. Hamza, though a poet, was not an argumentative man. He merely pointed to the Kaaba with a shrug of explanation. 'When I hunt the desert at night I know that God is not kept in a house.' It was simply said. Then Hamza planted his two legs firmly and regarded them all for a moment. 'The religion of my nephew is my religion. His God is my God. Strike me who dares.' Nobody moved except to get out of his way as he went in search of Mohammad.

A short time later another man with a sword in his hand and murder in his mind also went in search of Mohammad. He would end Islam at a stroke. He was Omar ibn al-Khattab and he was so tall he seemed to be stretched. It was said that he could mount his camel in one running stride, which was just as well because he was then an adventurous young man who made his living smuggling spices and stones across the border with Byzantium. He also had the bad temper of his camel.

The Prophet was praying by himself at Arqam's house, unarmed and undefended, when Omar came battering through the streets. I ran ahead to warn him, expecting him to be as frightened as I was at my news. But he scarcely stirred: 'God will choose the time when Omar ibn al-Khattab comes to me,' he said.

I could see Omar through the window, his sword out, his great height descending on the house. 'God has chosen' I said, 'for he is here now.'

I looked round for a weapon but there was nothing in the house except a pan of hot water on the fire. I got the pan and went slopping with it to the door. Then the Prophet stood up, more I think to restrain me than to protect himself. 'Thank you, Bilal,' he said, taking the hot water from me, 'but if this is the time God has chosen for me, even boiling oil wouldn't help me.' At least I think that's what he said, but don't hold my poor memory too dearly. Nowadays when you say what the Prophet said it becomes religion.

Omar wasn't fifty paces from the door – which weren't forty by his legs – when an old man stepped out in front of him. I thought it was a beggar, for men beg at the most inopportune times, and in spite of his anger, Omar was known as a generous man. But this time he gave nothing away but his violence. He lifted the old fellow up and shook him, shouting and swearing by every dead woman in the graveyard that he would kill *her* – which was, to my relief, different from killing *him*. Then Omar turned round and rushed back the way he had come as if the devil himself was hauling him in.

I knew that the day was not over yet. Omar was not a man who left anything, even the killing of a prophet, half done, so I waited near the window pretending to be lost in grammar. Arqam had come in – at least now there were three of us – but to be sure to have something in my hand I kept the water boiling. I wanted to get Hamza but he was off in the desert. We were, I suppose, in a state of siege.

An hour later I saw him coming again, sword still drawn, filling the road. Without any instruction I shut and bolted the door. The Prophet came behind me. 'Why shut the door, Bilal?' he asked. 'To save you from murder, Prophet of God,' I said. But he looked at me with a quiet eye. 'A Prophet may not shut his door, Bilal. Open it if you fear God.'

Mohammad stood in the middle of the room, waiting. I heard the hilt of Omar's sword beating on the door. But prophecy does as prophecy knows best, so I did what I was told and opened the door. Omar ibn al-Khattab stooped to come in. What I saw then I could not believe. Omar looked at the Prophet, looked at me, looked at Arqam and looked down at his sword. A great emotion struggled in him; pain changed his face; he undid his shirt as if to offer his heart. 'I declare there is no God but God and that you, Mohammad, are the Messenger of God.'

In that moment as surely as Christ had a Paul, Mohammad had an Omar. Indeed, when we talk about 'conversions' with either Paul or Omar we might be better off talking about 'revolutions', for such was the result of both these conversions. Both men started out hell-bent, Omar to murder the Prophet and Paul to kill Christians. Paul, they tell me, even held the coats of those who stoned Stephen, their first martyr, which is as near the fire as you can get. Yet God plucked both men back from the brink, saving them to become the great organizers of religion.

I saw, as I've related, only the extremes of Omar's conversion, its worst start and its best finish. I did not see the miracle of what happened in the hour between. My information is from Khabbab, the blacksmith who was there, and is as true as his own steel.

The man who stopped Omar on the road was not a beggar, as I had thought, but a merchant, some say a wine merchant, for God sends you Pharisees and sinners when you least expect them.

'Why is your sword out?' the old man had asked.

'To kill the fraud who has set himself over the gods,' Omar had replied.

'Then first go home and kill your own sister,' said the old man.

Such old men are oracles at the best of times and Omar only half understood him, but it was enough to provoke the rage I saw from the window. Omar loved his sister and the old man's hint of mystery concerning her made his madness madder.

He rushed back and lurked around her door. He heard voices and caught what he thought were some demented words. With one gallop, he kicked the door down, this seven-foot apparition of wrath with the lightning, his sword, flashing around his head. Inside, he saw his sister, Fatima, her husband, Saeed, and my witness, Khabbab. Fatima tried to hide a piece of paper underneath her skirt. Omar struck her a terrible blow in the face and as she fell back he plucked the paper from between her knees.

Omar did not know, as only the Prophet knew, that his sister had become a secret convert and what he held in his hand was a page of Sura 20 of the Koran, a sura of such beauty and mystery that no one can yet give a name to it. Its meaning is best left alone, for it is untranslatable and beyond all your poetry.

اَللّٰهُ لَاۤ اِلٰهَ اِلَّا هُوَ لَهُ الۡاَسۡمَاۤءُ الۡحُسۡنٰى

Omar stood with this verse in his hand and looked at his sister hiding in her husband's arms with the blood running on her face. He struck his head against the wall in guilt. 'What have you done to me?' he said, which is both a ridiculous and a moving question. Fatima, who was biting on her own blood, was too frightened to answer. Omar held out the paper to her as an excuse for her forgiveness. 'Read it to me,' he said, 'If it is worth our falling out, then read it to me.'

But Fatima's fingers failed her, so Khabbab, who could twist iron into the wing of a bird, took the page and read. As Omar listened, a slow deep wonder possessed him. He stared at the reader's lips in astonishment as he heard the Word of God spoken. He told me himself that suddenly a great sweetness flowed up through him and he trembled from head to foot.

Such was the conversion of Omar who this day leads all Islam.

Bilal
tells of
the Year
of Grief

It is called the Year of Grief. In that year everything failed us, and disasters fell in such heaps that even our faith was thrown into confusion. We looked to Heaven asking in what moment we had offended God. To be sure, in the six years of the Prophet's mission, we had grown a little and were now a hundred. A hundred is not many among the populations of the world, but once we were only ten. I like nothing more in my old age than to lean on my stick in Damascus and watch the Moslems in crowds go by. Thirty years ago we could all gather around one candle, but now God has multiplied each one of us by a million. I am glad to be still on the ground although I can tell you that in the Year of Grief I often wished I were under it.

First Khadija died. For twenty-five years she had been the Prophet's one wife and, as I've told you, in the first days she was his one believer. She had held him in her arms in the terror of the early revelations, she had shared all her wealth with him, shared even in its giving away. In the mystery of herself, she was the Mother of the Believers.

Suddenly, in a day, she was dead and we hurried her to her grave before night, our own Khadija.

Next Abu Talib died. He had lived a life hung between love and loss. He loved Mohammad yet died in idolatry, unable to shake off the dead religion of the dead. His fathers had shaped him too thoroughly. Yet he was the Prophet's support. I think perhaps God, who is the best plotter, chose Abu Talib's idolatry for him – because by staying in the dark he could more effectively defend the light. Had Abu Talib joined us he would have been cast out with us. Where then was the support? By being one of them he could be two of us and – although you may think I speak blasphemy – when I die I hope to be half as near God as Abu Talib.

With his last breath, he called the Lords of Mecca to one side of his bed and Mohammad, the Messenger of God, to the other side. He tried to make peace between them across his dying body. But it was not within Mohammad's power to allow any peace with idolatry. When he asked them to worship the One God only, they clapped their hands to prevent his words entering their ears. Abu Talib died in noise and sorrow.

The Prophet was silenced. His worst enemy, his uncle Abu Lahab, succeeded his best friend as the leader of the family of Hashim. Even his relatives, his blood and bone, were separated from him and the loud mouth of Abu Lahab, the Father of Flame, was the only authority on manners and religion. Abu Lahab defended the gods, al-Lat, Manat and al-Uzza, as if they were his own women and every morning he told them how pregnant and pleasing they were.

Poor fool, his worship was his last kick and the rage he turned on the Prophet became the very furnace he threw himself down into – he died, red-faced and swollen, in one of his angers and his soul now burns as a bonfire of warning to others. Even when he was still alive, God had judged his soul and reserved his room in Hell for him. In Sura 111, the Sura called 'Flame', God pointed at him.

> Perish the hands
> Of the Father of Flame
> Perish he.
>
> Neither his wealth
> Nor his profits
> Will avail him
>
> He will be burnt
> In a fire
> Of blazing flame.

His wife Awra was as bad as himself. As a child I remember her coming out under a white parasol to see the slaves corrected. I was afraid of her. Her later sport was tying bundles of thorn together with ropes of fibre and burning them at Mohammad's door. God did not divorce husband from wife in Hell; he put her with him.

His wife will be laden
With thorns
For burning.

A rope of fibre
Will be twisted about
Her neck.

I am sorry for them. They seemed to have had the devils called Legion cast into them and suffered like the two thousand pigs Christ caused to run and be drowned in the lake at Gadara. Their only hope is in the blessing of proximity – they shared the same weather with the Prophet. God may yet forgive them, though it is neither within my aim nor my shot to guess about God.

Banned from assembly and forbidden to preach, Mohammad began to think of other places less cold of heart and wild of temper than Mecca. The man who was safe in God was no longer safe in the streets. He decided to try Taif, a hillside town rising above the heat of the desert, surrounded by fruit trees and gardens with innumerable bees and butterflies. In this pleasant place they worshipped the goddess al-Lat in the image of a tall white stone.

Mohammad set out on foot to Taif, seventy miles to the south. This one-time well-off merchant, whose camels once went swiftly, had so impoverished himself with good works that he had nothing left to travel on but his two shoes. He hardly had a scarf for his face against the blowing sand and only one patched shirt. Yet I never saw a man so magnificent in his clothes – a threadbare shirt is cloth of gold upon a prophet's back.

He went off only with Saeed, his adopted son. We tried to follow him but he sent us back. He wanted no retinue. We were frightened. In Arabia when you travel you chance dry wells, the wind, the sun, misadventure, your enemy and yourself.

We were right. In two weeks he was back, a wreck of himself, holding out his hand for water, his wounds still raw. He dragged his body over the last yards of sand. Silence hung like a stone around his neck. He went to his widower's bed without a word.

Saeed told us what had happened.

He had arrived safely in Taif and secured a meeting with the elders. They sat on cushions nibbling sweets and sipping wine. He asked to be taken in and to be allowed to preach. They watched him over the rims of their cups in condescension and anticipation of sport. They tried their logic on him, for Taif was a city sophisticated by a cool wine. 'If you are the Messenger of God,' they said, 'then you are an angel to whom we are not allowed to talk; if you are not the Messenger of God, then you are an imposter. In both cases we should not talk to you.'

In this dazzle of themselves, they stood up and put on their true natures – rocks and stones. They let loose a mob of innocents, children without reason, screaming and cheering, joyful in cruelty, mere infants to stone the Prophet of God back into the desert. That day, the Prophet said, was the worst day of his life.

Only one mercy was afforded him. A Christian slave named Abbas, who chanced to be working in the fields, took pity on him and brought him a bunch of grapes. How happy a man is Abbas to have gained Heaven with a bunch of grapes! What a lottery there is in life and accident in salvation! The road to Heaven may be as short as it is long. I do not know the road of Abbas, but I love him.

Bilal tells how the Prophet was given a city

They say that on the night of Taif many stars disappeared from the sky. They say that the Pleiades not only wept – which could be thought normal – but were also heard to sob, which is nonsense. I was watching the sky that night and heard nothing. The event was elsewhere and when it happened it was nearly as extraordinary.

One night, twelve men from Medina came through the moonlight to offer their city to Mohammad. I had never seen any of them before, nor were they expected; but they had good reason for coming. They needed Mohammad as their peacemaker. Medina was a city of two tribes, the Aws and the Khazraj, who were continually at war. In the heart of every Aws was a wound inflicted by a Kharzaj and in the heart of every Khazraj was an injury given him by an Aws. They had heard of the Prophet who preached brotherhood and now came to seek reconciliation through him. Mohammad's father and mother had died six years apart at Medina, so his dust was already mingled with theirs.

He listened patiently. They were offering him now what he had sought at Taif, a place to live in and speak in beyond the reach of persecution. But it is beneath the dignity of a prophet to grab. He insisted that they understand him and themselves. So he asked them to accept his missionary, Mosaab, who would open Islam to them, and then to return in one year if they were of the same mind.

Before that year was over we were all older by five. We were dying of suffocation. We wondered if the men of Medina would ever come back – whether they had even been or we had dreamed them. We were a sorry sight. Abu Lahab still thought that his whip alone could prove the existence of his gods. We lived walled up in houses. Some weakended in their faith, complaining that the Prophet by his stubbornness had sent away divine rescue – as if the men who came by moonlight were twelve angels and not a dozen Arabs. But Mohammad who knew his own people, both in their beauty and their blemish, knew that the invitation to Medina was not a rope dropped from Heaven, although he might use it to climb among men. It had to be tested for its strength, and it was.

They came back – to the day, to the hour –'stealing along as softly as sandgrouse', as Mosaab said, to the secret meeting place at Aqaba. Not twelve, but seventy-seven came; nearly as many as all of us in Mecca. When I saw so many, I thought it was a trap. We were very jumpy in those days. But then I heard a tinkle of jewellery and I knew they had some women with them, which was encouraging. Promises made in the presence of women are twice kept.

The men, and now women, from Medina repeated their request – that Mohammad come and live with them and mediate between them. There was a pause. None of us knew what we know now – that this short pause was indeed a great gap of time; the future of our world was in it, history, the gathering of nations, man's prospering in God, all were in it. Yet the event itself was only the turning of a prophet's head.

Mohammed asked them for a promise. History calls this promise the Pledge of Aqaba, as if it were done with blood, seals and oaths. What I heard was more like a gentle request. He asked them to assure him that they would worship the One God only, that they would not mistreat their women or kill their female children, that they would neither lie nor steal, that they would obey God's laws and protect him and the people that came away with him. He warned them also that if he came to live with them he could never be owned by them; his heart must be open to all people; he could not choose one tribe, one race or one colour.

Yet what was he really asking? I never heard words so softly spoken whose meaning was so blunt. He was asking them to make firewood of their gods, to expel themselves from the rest of Arabia, even to be ready to make war for him. They knew that God's law, as Mosaab had told them, meant sharing their property with others, even to a segment of the orange brought down from the tree.

They asked him only one question – 'What will we get in return?' and he answered them in one word only, 'Paradise.' He gave his hand to each man in his turn and to the women he gave a nod, for to touch the body of another man's wife would have been unseemly.

Such was the Pledge of Aqaba. It was exchanged in a dry river-bed among rocks, but I – and I'm only what you see, a black man from Africa – I think we were not in any one place that night but in the heart of God. From Aqaba forward Islam became a nation, and the Prophet of God became a law-giver.

The Hegira

Bilal tells of the flight to Medina

I, Bilal, was now a leader of men.

I smile as I tell you, but forgive me my sin of pride, for I was no ordinary leader. Indeed I can say, as few can, that I was a natural born leader. In the back of every slave's head is the idea of running away and I, Bilal, led by running away. Behind blew the hot breath of the Father of Flame and who wouldn't be a hero when he has the devil at his back?

We left Mecca for Medina in small groups, at intervals, at night, over several nights. Mohammad was everywhere; he inspected us, inspired us, planned and timed our departures. His greatest fear was a mass slaughter in the desert; we were not to collect; we must go separate ways until we were out of reach. I was given a group, six men, two women, three children. The Prophet carried one of the children the first mile, then he bade us go. I tell you, had I met a lion in the desert I would have out-clawed him. I was now a leader of men.

The distance between Mecca and Medina is two hundred and fifty miles. In the summer it is a journey of nine days or, with children, eleven. The space has been travelled for thousands of years by millions of people and the wind has blown the sand over the footprints of every one of those travellers. Except ours. We were different. We carried responsibility to God, not loads of merchandise. As long as clocks run in the world, our footprints will stay, clean-swept. For we were Day One of Year One; our journey, the Hegira, dates our calendar. Our very footsteps started time.

Though it was June and the worst part of the year for a journey, I have to admit it wasn't too difficult. The winds that we feared held off. We were not pursued. The stars gave us a clear road. On the fifth day we saw some nomads, three or four, hurrying on the horizon but in a minute they were out of sight. One of the children raised an ostrich and I chased him in the hope of eating him, but he ran me into the ground. And that was all.

Of course we had our small ailments. You don't travel in the desert in summer without a sting. All the children were sick, on and off, but they enjoyed riding our backs. One of the men had an infected foot. He had hidden it for three days and I saw it only in his eyes, not in his step. When he realized that I knew and before I could say a word he hurried his pace – the poor man must have been walking in fire – until he was far out in front of everyone, a small figure alone. We had to run after him and plead with him before he would let us even look at his foot. But he hopped into Medina with his hand on my shoulder.

Such was our Hegira, our flight from Mecca.

Meccan cavalry surround the pilgrims

Pilgrims under guard await the Truce of Hudeibiya

The spreading of Islam

Meccans attack Moslems: the Truce of Hudeibiya is broken

Marching on Mecca

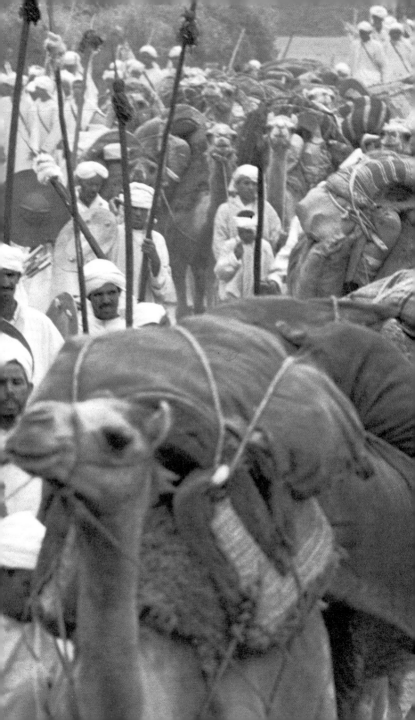

Marching on Mecca

Moslems enter Mecca

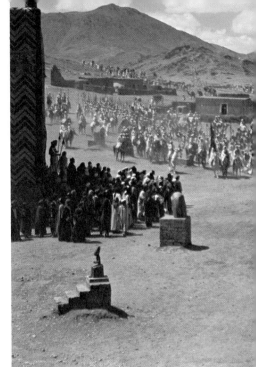

Moslem army within Mecca

The cleansing of the 'Kaaba': the burning of the idols

Bilal
tells of
the escape of
the Prophet

Yet our Hegira had a fear that we couldn't see. On the sixth day, Hamza found us. He had been riding the desert, frightening off lions, picking up the fallen, urging the backward, protecting and shepherding. He gave us the news we least wanted to hear – the Prophet had decided to stay on in Mecca until everyone was out.

Mohammad was, of course, keeping them away from us. When the Lords of Mecca had the queen of the hive in their hand why bother about the bees? So he walked openly among his enemies and murderers, almost inviting them to kill him, while we hurried ourselves to safety. His was a heroism that came from Heaven.

Several weeks passed before we heard all that happened, but the order of my story determines that I tell it to you now.

The Lords of Mecca had indeed made a plan to murder Mohammad, a plan with all the marks of a council of clever men. They would both kill and wash their hands of guilt in the same basin of blood – a crime at which government is often adept.

Seven men from seven tribes with seven spears were to strike into the body of Mohammad with a single stroke each. Because each spear was handled by a different tribesman, no one tribe could be made responsible for the murder and no one man might be tracked to his death, according to the custom. Blood spilt seven times is not easily avenged. It is more convenient to mop it up.

The solution of the seven spears was so subtle that I've heard it said the Devil himself proposed it. He came into the meeting of the Lords disguised as one of themselves. I wouldn't put it past him. The Devil loves to put on men's clothes and play men's parts. He is hard to place. He's either too serious or not serious enough, too clever or too clumsy; he rules in Hell but runs around earth in a variety of hats. Yet we must give the Devil his wit. It was surely an actor who fell from Heaven.

Devil or merchant, both failed. The spears were raised but none struck. The seven men burst into the Prophet's room at night when they thought him asleep. But he had got wind of the danger and that night put Ali, his cousin, into his place in the bed. Ali, the most modest man I know, smiled up at them and showed them that, although he lay in the bed, the bed was empty.

Mohammad was out of Mecca but still in danger. Abu Sofyan offered a reward of a hundred camels to anyone who would bring him, or his head, back to Mecca. Horse and camel were quickly run out and there was a great bustle of saddling and mounting. A hundred camels was a reward worth going for; besides, there was the sport of a man-hunt. As an ex-slave, I am in a position to tell you with what pleasure of hue and cry and with what frenzy a man will chase his own kind. No wild or timid beast gives him so much satisfaction as the two legs and flesh and blood of himself; yet, like Nimrod, he only chases himself into the fire.

Mohammad was wise enough not to try to make a run for Medina across the open desert. As soon as Abu Sofyan had thrown out his net of galloping men, the desert was death to him. Instead, God led him in the opposite direction, away from Medina, and hid him in a cave on Mount Thaur – for, as the Koran says, 'God is the best of plotters.' Abu Bakr was with him.

But a hundred camels is too tasty a dish to leave untried. By bad luck, Mecca had a tracker at this time, an Abyssinian as black as myself, who was the acknowledged master of the desert. They said he could track birds in the sky by smelling the air, and that he could follow footprints on rocks. His friends even claimed that, like a pig, he could see the wind. When everyone else was going forward, this genius insisted on going backwards: 'Mohammad is making the tracks, not I,' was all he said. His skill led him to the entrance of the cave of Thaur. Then he shrugged his shoulders and sat down – he had done his work, others could do the murder.

Umaya, Abu Jahl, and their manhunters were outside the cave.

'We are finished,' said Abu Bakr. 'There are twenty of them and only two of us.'

'You are wrong,' whispered the Prophet. 'God is also here. You, me and Him . . . therefore we are three.'

It was then that a spider swung down and began to work a web across the mouth of the cave; it was then that two white doves flew down with twigs in their beaks and began to nest by the entrance. Mohammad and Abu Bakr were crouching in the darkness of the cave, but neither of the small creatures of God and light had reason to fear.

Then Umaya, my old master, came up the rocks with his sword drawn and he, as always, frightened nature. The doves scattered and the spider disappeared into a crevice. But their work looked him in the face; its evidence was plain. No man could have entered the cave without breaking the web; birds do not nest among intruders. Umaya cursed the tracker, remounted his horse and rode off. The tracker too went his way and, I'm told, would never track a man again.

Perhaps these were natural happenings; spiders will spin and doves will nest. Yet that day the life of the Prophet of God hung on a spider's thread and religion rested on two doves.

They waited in the cave, in the presence of God, for three days until their pursuers had worn themselves out with useless searching. On the fourth night a Bedouin named Arqat, a pagan who knew the backways and empty spaces of the desert, brought them two riding camels and a bag of food. They groped down the mountain in darkness, the Prophet, the Companion and the pagan, and crept off to the west, still away from Medina. After two days, almost in sight of the Red Sea, they made a wide half-circle to the north avoiding all the known paths. Even then a pursuer found them but God caused his horse, the finest stallion in Arabia, to fall down. The man became a Moslem on the spot – or so the story tells itself.

Meanwhile, we watched and waited. Every morning we went out part of the way into the desert but the sun would drive us back after a few hours. These were the hottest days when nothing could move for long, when the traveller must halt and lie under a cloth until the sun had passed over his head. For a week, how well I remember it, we talked only in whispers.

Then, suddenly, a little after midday, there was a shout and everyone was running. It was a Jew, praised forever be his long sight, who saw them first – three distant, small figures bumping up and down on their camels, moving slowly in the heat. We ran into the desert to meet them, waving palm leaves, stumbling, falling, laughing in joy, shouting in victory. The Messenger of God had come to his city.

There are two great journeys in the history of religion: The Flight of the Jews from Egypt, the Exodus, and our Flight from Mecca, the Hegira. If there is a third, I can't think of it. The Hegira delivered Islam from its persecutors.

The Prophet came to his city on the 28 June 622, in the Christian Era; or in the year 4382 of the Jewish ancestry. But to us the Hegira begins our calendar. The Hegira happened in the Year One.

Bilal
tells of
a camel's
choice

Under the nearest palm tree, before he had even dismounted, the Prophet had to make his first decision of statecraft – because in his first step into his new city he was put in danger of dividing it. From every side voices were offering him lodgings. Such invitations were not all generosity. An important guest gives importance to his host and a man is often imprisoned in the hospitality he receives.

Salool, the hypocrite, was the most persistent. He took the reins of the camel, as if he could lead the Prophet of God away to his own ambition. 'I have the best house in Medina,' he said. 'Stay with me. I have gardens and I keep the best table.'

Mohammad was caught in a danger of choices – by pleasing one faction he would be rejecting another. But, as I've often observed, the most complicated men sometimes find the simplest solutions.

I saw a twinkle in the Prophet's eye as he patted his camel, Qaswa, on the neck. 'I cannot choose between so many welcomes,' he said, 'but Qaswa has proved so faithful to me on my journey that I'm inclined to leave the choice to her.' You should have seen the looks of bewilderment on every face, except for Qaswa herself, who chewed away in animal meditation. The Prophet raised his riding stick in a gesture that ended one uncertainty and started another. 'Where my camel chooses to stop there I will stay and there I will build my Mosque.'

He dismounted and smacked his camel on the rump. We all followed the heavy, ugly, light, mysterious, gainly, ungainly, lumbering animal into the depth of the oasis. I won't say that we hung on to her tail, but I will say that we turned with her head. We did not know it then, but that camel had both our place of habitation and the Prophet's grave under her hump. The Prophet was leaving the most important political decision of his life to a beast of burden.

Qaswa went a fair distance before she stopped. But the stop was only a shuffle. She sniffed around, ate a leaf, scratched, backed a step, and went on. We let out the breath of suspense and followed after. I overheard Salool say the first of his many mixed compliments to the Prophet. 'He's cleverer than I thought,' he said. 'A choice made by a camel can offend no one.'

I followed Qaswa – four steps to her two. Every camel, like every dog, has its day and I've no doubt that they'll be talking about this camel and this day even at the end of the world. When Bucephalus, Alexander's war horse, and Incitatus, the horse that Caligula made a senator of Rome, are forgotten, they'll still remember Qaswa, the camel of Mohammad, the steed of the Hegira. With her white coat, her expansive nostrils and her philosopher's gaze, she was camel to perfection. But every perfection must have a flaw and Qaswa's flaw was on her left ear; it had been chewed up in a camel fight when she was young. Elsewhere she was unmarked.

Suddenly she found the place, a small field bounded by five trees. But she had not done yet with her dramatics or emptied her bag of tricks. More was in store. She buckled her knees, knelt, got up, turned and sniffed the spot, whisked the flies off with her tail, looked north towards Jerusalem and south towards Mecca, emitted a low bubbling sound and knelt again – this time letting down the weight of her body – then, thump! all of Qaswa was down. She stretched out her neck and laid her chin on the ground. She had chosen.

Mohammad stood over his resting camel and declared in a loud voice. 'Here I will stay. Here you will bury me. Here I will build my Mosque.'

Bilal
tells of
the building
of the
Mosque

Work began at dawn. Mohammad himself drew the first line of the Mosque with the point of a lance, working between the five tall palm trees. These trees were so finely spaced that it seemed God had put them up for our purpose, to be the pillars of our Mosque, and indeed it was God who guided the camel to this place.

When we saw the first line drawn and the first sod turned, we went wild with the joy of the work. We dug with our feet and shaped with our hands. We made the bricks, carried stones, sawed wood, stirred mortar, levelled ground, cleared scrub, dug trenches, climbed ladders, hoisted baskets, tied and hammered to our hearts' content. We did it all with such lightness that those who saw us said we were dancing.

Mohammad carried bricks and climbed ladders with the best. Although only just in from a terrible journey that would have put other men into bed for a week, he refused even to sit down. Everywhere he went he had a run of young children after him, all eager to help, but spoiling the work. I once tried to free him from their pestering, but he turned his wit on me. 'Help poor Bilal,' he said. I had to go up a tree to escape the swarm of them, while he stood there laughing and wiping the sweat off his face. Then he lifted a toddler in his arms and put a half-brick into his small hands. He carried the toddler to the wall and helped him lay the brick. 'You can now say you helped me build my Mosque,' he said and let him down to stagger back to his mother with a grin bigger than his whole face.

No one could make him rest, not even Hamza, who got a flip of a prophet's cloak and dust in his face when he begged him to sit down. So we made the best of a lost battle and sang a song about it.

If we sat down
While the Prophet worked,
God would say
That we had shirked.

He had, I'm sure, good reasons for working the way he did, for he was always teaching us. 'Work is a prayer,' he would say. 'God loves the hand of a workman,' he would say.

He forbade us to overload the animals, to ride two on a donkey or to over-estimate the strength of the camel. He had a quick eye against cruelty, and woe to any man who hurt an animal without cause – he might feel the frown of a prophet.

And so the Mosque was built.

Bilal makes his first Call

No doubt there were more handsome buildings – none of us were architects – and I can't say that I've ever stood under the dome of the Church of the Holy Wisdom in Byzantium, but what we made, we made; a house within our worship. As we rested on the floor after our labours gazing up at the soft dappled light filtering through the palm thatch of the roof, Hamza had his own fine words for our handiwork. 'It's like the cradle of Moses,' he said, and the comparison pleased the Prophet. Indeed, it was a cool place, refreshing to the spirit and pleasing to the eye, a green shade.

But although the Mosque was built, it was still incomplete.

It was Ali, I think, who told us it needed one more touch. 'We're missing something . . . something high up there,' he said, pointing to the roof, 'some signal . . . a way to call the people in.'

'We could run a flag up,' suggested Ammar.

In a moment we were all going backwards and forwards, up and down, arguing how best to call the Faithful to their prayer. The Prophet sat through it all with his arms folded, neither taking himself out of nor putting himself into the question.

'Why not use a bell?'

'The Christians have bells.'

'A drum?'

'There's too much blood in a drum.'

'A horn, like the Jews? That's a strong note.'

'There's too much of the animal left in a horn.'

'A trumpet?'

We fell silent. A flag, a bell, a drum, a ram's horn, a trumpet? Nobody was satisfied. A bell jangles the ear, a trumpet splits the head, a drum thumps up the blood and a flag goes too far in the other direction – it would never wake a sleeper.

Then I saw Abdullah Bin Zaid, one of the Helpers, coming forward shyly, inch by inch, so bashful that he seemed frightened of stirring the air – he who, in the next minute, was going to stir the world. I saw at once that he had something to say, so I gave him my space near Mohammad.

'I had a dream, Messenger of God,' he began, 'and in this dream I heard the human voice calling us to prayer . . .' He tailed off as if he thought no one was listening. 'An ordinary human voice.'

I looked quickly at Mohammad and saw that tears had come into his eyes. He leaned towards Abdullah. 'Yes. It will be so. Your dream was from God. It will be as you say . . . the human voice.' He spoke so gently that I knew his word was the last word.

It was settled. But what voice, whose, and how spoken? A soft voice, a sweet voice, a bellowing voice? My mind was racing in the possibility of voices – a child's, a woman's, an old man's, a soldier's, a singer's, a scholar's – when I felt, and I saw, the Prophet's hand on my shoulder.

'Your voice, Bilal.'

I did not at first take in what he said. When I felt his hand on my shoulder I jumped up without knowing why. My old instincts as a slave, which are hard to lose, had taught me to start moving even before understanding. I saw every face in the Mosque turned to me and then it dawned. But I who was to become the voice of Islam had nothing to say.

Saeed reached up and put his hand into mine and said something that still makes me cringe with pride. 'I wish I had such a gift to give to Islam.' Forgive me for repeating a compliment to myself; I say it because Saeed, whom I loved and who gave so much, said it.

Then Mohammad stood up and looked me in the face as only he could look at a man. But I have to admit that he said less than Saeed. 'You have the best voice, Bilal. Use it.'

'Messenger of God, what will I say?'

'Praise God, declare His Messenger, exhort to prayer, praise God. That is all. And all is enough.'

When the crown of his life is thrust upon a man, he does not always want it. Even Mohammad himself when he received his call hid under blankets. I don't compare myself, only to say that I, too, wanted blankets. But there were none, no place to hide, no avoidance.

'Go up now and call them from up there,' the Prophet said.

I looked to where he was sending me, a mud roof near the Mosque. You all have seen your minarets . . . how graceful the steps, how secure the balconies, how good their elevation. A muezzin can keep his breath in the climb and the first glint of the horizon – not looking for the difference between a white thread and a black thread – tells him the time of a new day. But when I climbed to make the first call, I had to go up as best I could, by pulling myself up, hand, belly, knee and foot. And even then, I was still below the palm trees. But worse, when I got up on that roof, I had nothing in my head. I had no one to copy and no words, either to remember or forget.

Yet below me the upturned faces.

God knows that I, Bilal, the first muezzin can tell you about faces and how looking up to you, they lift you. The climbs were often dizzy, but the faces would never let you fall.

That first time, with not one word to say, I looked back. Mohammad was near the third pillar, with Abu Bakr and Omar standing beside him – Omar so tall that he seemed to be halfway up the tree. The Prophet raised his hands towards me in a lifting gesture, both encouraging me and telling me to begin.

'Praise God, declare His Messenger, exhort to prayer, praise God,' he had said. That was to be the order.

I turned away and thought. Then I threw back my head into the depth of my voice.

> God is most great. God is most great.
> I witness that there is no god but God.
> I witness that Mohammad is the Messenger of God.
> Come to prayer.
> Come to prayer.
> Come to good work.
> God is most great. God is most great.

Every day now, five times a day, through all Islam you hear those words. Yet I, who first spoke them, do not know where I found them. The Prophet had given me their order certainly, and when you know the shape you are more than halfway to the words. Yet they still must be thought. Did he when he gestured with his open hands give me the words? For I'll never believe I made them up myself. I believe the words were cast into me.

'*Allahu Akbar*.' 'God is most great.'

When I came down Mohammad brought me to sit nearest him. The people flowed around us; a bunch of children came to giggle and run away. We made a fine pair, the Prophet of God sitting with the son of the slave. For a long time he said nothing and I admit that I, too, was lost in a mystery of my own. Then he had to go to lead the prayers. He rose and took me in his arms. 'Bilal, you have completed my Mosque,' was what he said.

Thereupon, in the company of all those people who had come into the Mosque in answer to my call, I prostrated myself before God. I, Bilal, had achieved my life.

PART TWO

Mohammad's first action in Medina was to fulfil his promise to heal the wounds of the quarrelling tribes.

He negotiated a treaty that in the light of Arabian tradition was revolutionary: it replaced loyalty to the tribe and family with loyalty to the religious community. 'Each Moslem is a brother of every other Moslem. Among Moslems there are no tribes or races.' This abolition of the tribal hold was almost a change of nature for the Arab.

Mohammad, working by persuasion and moral force rather than by decree, set out to make Medina the perfect city. The Koran was still being revealed, and where it touched human legislation it was, of course, absolute and the 'penalties imposed by God' were very strictly enforced. They could not be altered or reduced without peril.

On the other hand, the lesser man-made laws – the edifice of the Perfect City – were administered mildly. They covered all aspects of everyday life, from dealings in the marketplace to the management of households, and Mohammad used them to teach rather than to punish, to reform rather than to avenge.

His translation of much of the spiritual message of the Koran into social reality showed Mohammad's genius as a law-giver. He expressed human sympathies that in their time, the seventh century, were astonishing. Many of his social ideas were not realized institutionally in western civilization until the nineteenth and twentieth centuries.

Mohammad's greatest fear, which he included in his fear of God, was doing any injustice to man, woman or creature.

Bilal
tells of
Mohammad
the Law-giver

In Medina, Mohammad became the most fortunate of prophets because he could practise what he preached. But he was also in a vulnerable position, for the men who had listened to his sermons could now judge his actions.

Mohammad was not like Moses, lit by flashes of lightning, existing in the mind's eye, seen brilliantly one moment and darkly the next. This prophet could be met face to face, greeting to greeting, at any odd hour in the streets of Medina. Nor was he like Jesus – remembered. A thousand witnesses would cry me dead if I tried to limit Mohammad to as many as even four memories, even to the blessed remembrances of Matthew, Mark, Luke and John.

Mohammad lived in the common light of day, a full-length man. I know, because, as I've said, every morning on my way to the first call I would knock on his door to wake him up. Often he would come out to me still blinking and rubbing off sleep, poking around with his foot to find his sandals in the morning dark. Certainly he was not finding them by inspiration, only by a bare foot. Nor did he rise like a lord expecting everyone else to be out of bed before him. He led by love. He listened and advised rather than decreed and governed. Being a shy man he rarely spoke first, and then with many graces and courtesies. Often he would sit at the back of a discussion, leaning forward eagerly as if he were a young man learning. He was never rude in disagreement, and although he often seemed short in his replies, it was because he was thinking in a quicker way. His book of logic was the human heart and he preferred it to the libraries some men carry in their heads.

Although he received Heaven's word, he himself denied infallibility, placing his opinion no higher and no lower than that of the last speaker. But we knew better. What he said was so pure and logical that we made it our law.

Too much respect put Mohammad into uncomfortable silences and we who were closest to him learned to hide our awe in questions, in familiarity and humour. Often I saw him suffering from praise. 'I am but a man . . . I am but a man . . .' he would mutter to those well-meaning people who thought to please him by congratulating him on the Heaven that is surely his, '. . . and I don't know what God has in store for me.'

Although he was the highest among us all, he was also, in the possessions of the world, among our lowest. He was not a fanatic or a self-starver. If he went to bed hungry many nights it was only for reasons of the belly – he had given his food to someone he felt might be hungrier than himself.

What have since become our laws were often his living example. When we saw the good in his actions we made them our doctrines. We remembered nearly everything he said; very little slipped away, and whatever fell from his lips we gathered up. Already men spend their days and nights repeating his sayings. But I fear embroidery and addition. I have my own test for the proof of his sayings. Unless I heard them from him himself, I judge them, however brilliant or surprising they may seem, by their plainness. For Mohammad never said more than the common sense of Islam.

However rich in faith, the Moslems arrived destitute in Medina and soon became an economic burden on the city. Their possessions in Mecca had been confiscated and used to enrich the great caravan to Syria. This caravan, with the proceeds from the stolen property literally on the backs of the camels, passed only seventy miles to the west of Medina. After considerable hesitation, Mohammad decided to seize the caravan. He received 'permission' by Koranic revelation to wage a war of self-defence.

In January 624, year 2 of the Hegira, Mohammad set out with a small army of 300 men. But the Meccans had news of his march; the caravan escaped and at the wells of Bedr Mohammad found himself faced with an overwhelming force of a thousand well-armed, well-mounted men.

The Moslems won the Battle of Badr against all the odds and this obscure skirmish in the desert became one of the decisive battles of the world. Had they lost, the tiny nation of Islam would have been wiped out.

Bilal
tells
about his
battles

The heaviest load I ever lifted was my sword. I was no good in the killing and however hard I tried I could never make my sword my cunning. I could never measure a man or strike my full weight or reach my height in the thrust. Both Hamza and Ali did their best to teach me; in fact the day before we set out for Badr, Ali fenced with me behind the Mosque all morning, showing me the strokes and the steps. I got my feet easily enough – even Hamza complimented me on the sway of my body and Ali said that I had good 'drift' – but my arms wouldn't answer my legs. Not that it mattered, faith blew us forward and, as often as not, the men in front melted away. I sometimes think we won those early battles with our eyes.

You may indeed say that Bilal was at Badr. Had I been dead before I got there I would still have been present. For the Prophet chose my cry in my tortures, 'One God', to be the battle-cry of the army.

He knew that my talents were not in blood so he gave me other duties and great responsibilities. I was put in charge of the food supply of the army. When you consider our number, a mere three hundred men, a handful in the history of campaigns, my work may seem light to you. But at this time we were so poor that feeding even three hundred men on the march needed an act of God. But I managed it without miracles, foraging through Medina, begging, borrowing, bullying. I was as quick to see a speck of corn as any scratching hen, I grant, but the stories that I would follow a line of ants to rob from them is an exaggeration. I did, however, imitate the ant – when you have next to nothing every crumb is worth carrying.

In the end, the proof was in the result. No Moslem fell at Badr because of an empty belly. Yet I know that it wasn't my poor scrounging that filled them up – that day Heaven gave them their soup.

For before we set out God had revealed Himself in clear terms. He did not turn us loose. We fought only by permission and only in self-defence and only in a limited way.

Fight in the way of God
Against those who fight against you . . .
Against those who drove you out of your homes,
Fight.
But start no war
For God loves not the makers of war.
And if your enemy cease his aggression
Then you may fight no more.

Once in arms, the Prophet proved himself as good a general as ever shied away from war. He himself gave us our discipline and our order of standing. We were a new sight in desert battle, which had always been fought in loose formations and in small, isolated, bloody whirl-pools. But Mohammad stood us tightly together. He made every man part of a fortress so that one increased the other; four men became five; sword, shield, arrow, javelin and spear worked in articulation. Yes, he was a general. We have used his line in all our battles and suffered only when we changed from it.

Mohammad retired to his tent early to pray and never looked out on the fight, but before he went he gave us a promise. It was nothing less than the reward of death. 'Today Paradise is under the shadow of swords . . .' he said, ' . . . and he who dies today will be carried up to Heaven by angels.' But he conditioned the promise. The wounds of death must be on the face of the body, not in the back – except when wounds are got bravely in the turn of a mêlée or in the tactic of retreat; then a wound in the back is as good as a wound in the face.

I tell you all this to tell you how exactly, in what detail, we were led. We fought by principle, not by lust, however difficult it may be to avoid lust in battle. For blood runs to the head of the fighting man long before it gushes to the ground and he who flies forward, wades back. All is in the location of the blood. Mohammad tried to reduce war, giving it rules and conventions, seeking to impose humane agreements on its brazen inhumanity. But he could not stop war because, like Joshua, the son of Nun, it was forced upon him.

Again he chose me; again I was his speaker. It was a January evening and a cold wind was blowing across from Persia. In all our times together I never knew him so indrawn and so quiet. I had to lean my

Bilal climbs the 'Kaaba'

Bilal climbs the 'Kaaba'

Bilal calls to prayer

head to hear him. Then his voice fell away into silence and I heard only
I remember – two dogs barking at each other in the distance.

The next day I stood shouting. I stood with my back to the trees of
Medina facing the desert where we would march. There was one small
fleecy cloud in the sky and if there was a creature in that cloud, he
heard me. For I was proud of what I said.

'These are the Rules of War:
You may not hurt a woman, or a child.
You may not harm the man who works in the field.
You may not harm old men or take advantage of cripples.
You may not cut down fruit trees.
You may not take a drink of water without permission or food
without payment.
You may not tie up a prisoner or force him to walk while you ride.
The enemy who surrenders to you must be treated kindly by you.
You must beware of harming children.'

Twice he told me to warn about the children.

And so we left Medina, three hundred and fourteen men, with
seventy camels and only two horses. Against us, out of Mecca, marched
a force of a thousand men with seven hundred and fifty camels and a
hundred horses. We wrapped the bark of trees around our bodies for
armour while they stepped into iron and mounted over us like towers
on horseback.

But we won.

I must now defend myself against the charge that I, in cold blood,
killed a prisoner. Cold blood there was certainly, for my blood always
ran cold, summer like winter, when I saw that man. He was Umaya,
my former owner, who had whipped me to the moment of death.

It was late in the evening when we had won and opened our ranks
for the pursuit. Prisoners were being brought in, yes. But between Bilal
and Umaya there could be no quarter as between Umaya and Bilal,
twelve years before, there had been none. For a moment I was only
aware of blindness, blinding sun, a memory, and although my blood
was cold my rage was hot.

He was on horseback, I on foot, he armoured, I bare; but I had the advantage of surprise. He did not expect me as I broke through the crowd surrounding him. He was, I admit, in the act of surrendering and had he kept his head he could easily have kept his life. He had only to drop his sword and, at the worst, my friends would have held me back. But perhaps he couldn't. Perhaps it was not possible for him to surrender to his one-time slave. If so, he collaborated in his own death and, like a fool, spent his blood to pay for his pride.

He turned his horse at me, calling me slave again. I should have laughed at him, but I didn't. I took him seriously for the last time.

As I told you, I was no good at measuring a man, but now I did and foot, thigh, arm and eye blasphemed together. As he raised himself to strike he showed a chink in his armour, a gash across his belly no more than an inch wide, no thicker than the moon when it is two days new. He fell in my first thrust. I heard the sweep of his sword passing my head, as if it were a sound far away, like a migrating bird.

I had to step back to avoid the fall of his body. I swear to you that for a moment I wanted to pick him up, as though it were still my work to take care of him; only when they rolled him over and I saw his face again did I realize what I had done.

I felt filled with a great anxiety. For bred into every slave, or nursed into him in the milk of his mother or thrown to him with his first mess of slave food, is the fear of striking back, of returning the blow of his owner. For the punishment is pitiless. Now I stood over that owner, my sword wet with him, my whole body gnawed by the rat of instinct.

Many nights since I have lain awake, remembering that terrible minute, asking questions of the dark. Did I, Bilal, exact a vengeance God denied me? Had I a cause? Was revenge allowed me? Was he a prisoner or a man still in arms? Had he struck at me in his self-defence or had I killed him in my own? Was I guilty by my fury or innocent by his? What held my sword that day, his future or mine?

My friends around me and around the corpse of Umaya congratulated me. But I know that there were no witnesses to our conclusion. I and Umaya were alone.

HISTORY PAGE THREE

In January 625, year 3 of the Hegira, a new Meccan army
led by Abu Sofyan appeared before Medina. Again
Mohammad was outnumbered: three to one in men,
and a wild fifty to one in horsemen.
But again he chose battle, trusting in the strength of his
cause and in the help of angels. He engaged the enemy
on the foothills of Uhud, a small rocky mountain three
miles north of the city.
The Battle of Uhud went the way of Badr, victory and
the confusion of enemies – up to the last hour. But this
time Mohammad won too soon, and, then, only
incompletely. While his elated men were gathering in the
spoils of their victory, a powerful force of cavalry
concealed behind a hill swept down on their backs. The
Moslems were scattered and Mohammad barely escaped
with his life – even the Faithful thought him dead. The
valiant Hamza was killed.
But the Meccans, who were fighting for the honours of
a battle rather than the winning of a war, failed to
follow up their advantage. They could have taken
Medina unopposed; instead they rode for
home singing victory songs.

Bilal
tells of
the day of
Uhud

War, we learned at Uhud, is a contradiction and a swing – now up-backwards, now down-forwards. A battle does not decide who is right, only who is left standing. The sword is illiterate and has never yet written one page of religion. The importance of war is what happens before and after, before the saluting and after the blooding.

At Uhud, they were left standing and we – surprised, dismayed, tamed – sent scrambling for our lives. They had won. But what, in the happiness of their victory, did they do? On that field of thorns and stones, their undisputed field, they planted crops for themselves in Hell. For they stripped and mutilated the dead. They vented themselves upon nothing, the ears, noses and organs of the dead. In the heap of victory they were the first worms.

But why, why mutilate the dead? Why dishonour the body? Why this? I've heard of the Greek Achilles who dishonoured the corpse of his enemy by dragging it in the dust behind his chariot at Troy. I find no reason. Perhaps they think to make the dead the scarecrows of the future. Perhaps they hold the fear – as I do myself – that after any battle the dead are the final judges of the day. If so, it is the weak devouring the strong. Perhaps they fear – as I do myself – that after any battle death's grin is indeed the last laugh. I cannot tell.

I promised you contradiction and you shall have it. We held the sky over Uhud although we ran on its ground. It was not the men of two cities, faith and unfaith, who fought at Uhud – the contention was between God and us. In clear statement, in Verse 166 of Sura 3, God revealed to His Messenger that he brought us to defeat at Uhud as a trial that we must pass through.

> What you suffered on the day
> The two armies met
> Was ordained by God.
> He tested you that day
> In the strength of your belief
> And He tried you in your faith.

At Badr, He excited us; at Uhud He sobered us. We had indeed broken ranks too soon, running when the Prophet was calling us back, thinking that Heaven would still help us even in our disobedience. But as young children are sometimes given hard lessons, so were we.

The price was high.

On the day of Uhud, Hamza fell. A skilled javelin thrower, an Ethiopian like myself, had been bribed by Hind – offered not only his freedom, but his weight in silver and his height in silk – for one throw of his javelin. His name was Wahshi and all that day he wriggled between the fighting men but took no side with any of them. He sought Hamza.

Hamza was striding forward through a lane of his own hacking, invincible in his walk, when his murderer suddenly rose from the dead behind him. He threw his one throw and left the field.

In my heart I pity Wahshi. Freedom to a slave is a bribe hard to refuse. But he never wore the silk or spent the silver, he took his freedom and went with it into the desert, hiding even from his own name. Years later he came to the Prophet, who forgave him and took his hand. But then Mohammad asked him to leave as his presence pained him.

On the day of Uhud, Hind's beauty got itself a bloody face. She cut Hamza's liver out of his side, put it to her teeth and chewed it, thereby mutilating her own fair looks forever. Perhaps the poet is right – women are too cruel to be allowed on a battlefield.

On the day of Uhud, the Prophet of God escaped death only by a missed stroke. He fell to the ground wounded by a stone. Ibn Qamia, the sharpest swordsman of Mecca, stood over him. It was an easy, effortless kill but suddenly, in a wild running of the blood, ibn Qamia, who was a man of slow blood and no emotion, became clenched with hatred. He lifted his sword too high and came down too soon. For all his reputation for accuracy, in that moment he couldn't have driven goats through a gate.

I watched it all happen clearly, even slowly, as if the instant were an hour. I flung myself full length at ibn Qamia, my sword and myself slithering along the ground. I think I touched him on the foot, but I've never been sure. Then we gathered around the Prophet, twelve of us, our swords like the bristles of a porcupine.

When it was over and Abu Sofyan had ridden away, the Prophet prayed over the dead, each in his turn. When night came he was still there, his lantern moving slowly among the corpses.

On the night of Uhud.

In spite of his defeat at Uhud, Mohammad's strength grew and Abu Sofyan realized his mistake in not occupying Medina. After two years of raid, ambush and skirmish, he returned to full-scale war. This time there would be no hesitation; he would carry the fight to the last Moslem. In February 627 he came north with ten thousand mounted men, an army it seemed impossible to oppose.

Even in their confidence in Heaven, the Moslems did not dare to venture out again. But Mohammad again showed his originality and skill as a strategist. With the advice of Salman, a freed Persian slave, he dug a ditch around the city too wide for horses to jump. Such a simple fortification was still so unusual in Arabian warfare that the Meccans did not know how to overcome it.

After twenty days of stalemate and single combat, a sudden storm blew down their tents and terrified their horses. Abu Sofyan raised the siege and went home; he had accomplished nothing. In the wind that scattered their enemies it was easy for the Moslems to find the hand of God.

Mohammad now saw his opportunity for peace and imposed it by an extraordinary show of moral force. He led his followers unarmed, without a bow or an arrow, towards Mecca on a pilgrimage. They were met by Abu Sofyan's cavalry at Hudeibiya but Mohammad showed them his empty hands and his clothes of pilgrimage.

A truce – the Truce of Hudeibiya – was concluded under a thorn tree. In early Moslem precedence, to have been present at the tree of Hudeibiya was the highest honour, implying faith, courage, commitment and a true Islam – surrender to God.

The principal term of the Truce was peace for ten years.

Bilal
answers
a lie

I've heard it said by some of the wits here in Damascus that Islam spreads itself with the sword. The fools. They think that religion is reaping; it is not. Religion is sowing. Only God does the reaping. Fear God.

Yet they still say it: 'Your Islam, your surrender to your God, is everyone else's surrender to your horses.' When I ask them to bring me one man or show me one town compelled to Islam by force they are silent. So I must be loud.

If a Moslem forces a conversion, he doesn't risk Hell. No. He is certain of Hell. For God's warning is short: 'There is no compulsion in religion.' When they accuse us of swords, I show them my stick. How can an old man's stick be quiet in a young man's world? Yet were I to tie a carrot to my stick and lead their donkeys to conversion – as legends say a Christian mass bell converted a pair of swans – I, Bilal, would be burned white in the fire. For as there is no compulsion in religion, there is no bribery either.

No sword, no threat, no twist, no broken bone, no bribe can bring a man to belief. Because deep within the prohibition against forced conversion is the very diamond of religion, beautiful and unbroken.

It is God, not man, who decides who will believe in Him. In the Sura of Jonah, Verse 100, God puts all mankind, even the wits here in Damascus, to that one question.

> No soul can believe
> Except by the wish of God,
> Will you then compel mankind
> Against their will to believe?

How then is Islam spread by the sword? But no matter how many times you prove an impossibility there will always be someone to say it is a certainty.

Though only a bare thorn, great fruit fell from the tree of Hudeibiya; though only a tree without leaves, it shaded thousands. But don't turn my metaphor into a miracle, even if the result of the Truce seemed like a miracle. For the first time we could go freely, from oasis to oasis, from well to well, speaking openly without fear of stoning or whipping or the camp dogs.

By word not sword, by invitation not compulsion, we persuaded men's hearts. This was the spread of Islam.

HISTORY PAGE FIVE

The Truce of Hudeibiya, agreed for ten years, lasted only two. It was broken by Mecca, though in an indirect way and without the knowledge of Abu Sofyan. Some tribesmen allied with the Meccans murdered some tribesmen allied with the Moslems. It was a small local affair but it was cause.

Mohammad marched on Mecca. Islam had spread so quickly in the period of the Truce that the Prophet now had a huge following. Ten thousand set out from Medina and were joined by other thousands from the tribes along the way. Arabia had never seen so great an army. Abu Sofyan, looking for the best in a hopeless situation, went alone to the Moslem camp. He tried to make terms but the days of compromise were past; so he made his peace with Mohammad and his surrender to Islam.

Bilal
tells of
the surrender
of Abu Sofyan

I had my first hint – broad as you like – that something unusual was happening when Abu Dharr, his eyes bulging, choked on his food and Omar's huge hands clenched. My back was to the event, so I turned.

There he was, our enemy of twenty years, our persecutor, our would-be destroyer, Abu Sofyan himself, walking among our campfires. He carried himself well, with the dignity and the quietness that we once so feared.

He stood at our fire, but none of us rose. Then he looked out over our thousands of fires, like stars fallen from Heaven, twinkling to the horizon. 'The kingdom of Mohammad has become very wide,' he said, almost curiously. This misconception was too much for me, so I corrected him: 'Mohammad is a prophet, not a king.'

Abu Sofyan nodded slowly as if lost in himself, then he spoke my name, 'Bilal.' He could have been naming me for another whipping, he spoke so softly. I looked up at him with old memory – you might say I struck him with my eye – and he turned away. I went past him into the tent where Mohammad was praying.

'Messenger of God,' I said, 'Abu Sofyan has come.' 'God chooses every man's time,' he said and gestured to me to bring Abu Sofyan in. He showed no sign of victory; he just covered his eyes with his hand. 'It is God who invites,' he said.

Ali went first, then Abu Sofyan, while Omar, who had put on a sword, and I brought up the rear. We were a small procession, but we were the fall of Mecca.

Abu Sofyan began with a proposition of terms . . . the truce to be continued, the Meccans to remain in arms, the Moslems to have rights of pilgrimage . . . But the Prophet cut him short. 'That time is past,' he said. 'It is too late for that.'

Then followed an exchange that I will never forget. Ali began it.

'Hasn't the day come for you, Abu Sofyan, to recognize that Mohammad is the Messenger of God?' Abu Sofyan looked down at the mat we were sitting on. His eyes seemed shut: 'Mohammad there is still doubt in my heart,' he said.

Omar was next and, as usual, decisive. 'If we were to cut off your head it would remove your doubts.'

I had never argued with Omar but now I had to. I reached over and put my hand on his. 'There can be no compulsion in religion,' I said. The Prophet smiled and I could see he was pleased. But Abu Sofyan stared at me, as a child might who had never seen a black man.

'You, black slave,' he said, 'you are the best school.' He spoke to Mohammad again. 'If my gods were worthy of my worship they would have saved me before now.'

The Prophet replied by merely waiting. Then Abu Sofyan spoke out clearly, with no hesitation. 'I declare of my own free will and under no compulsion that there is no god but God and that you, Mohammad, are the Messenger of God.'

Such was the Islam, the surrender to God, of Abu Sofyan. And so, next morning, we carried on towards Mecca, our last mile, our happiest step.

Eight years after he had fled from Mecca by night,
Mohammad returned a conqueror. The city surrendered
without a fight.
Once more, Mohammad showed his tolerance. He shed
no blood and took no revenge. Not one door was
broken down.
The past was forgotten and the present forgiven.
In the name of the One God, he cleansed the Kaaba of its
360 gods. The idols were pulled down, broken up and
burned. This was the only fury of the conquest.
When the fire had burned out, Mohammad stood on the
steps of the Kaaba and declared the triumph of Islam:
'Truth has come and falsehood is fled away.'
Then he ordered Bilal to climb the black hangings of the
Kaaba and make his call to prayer high up on its roof.

Bilal
tells how
he climbed
the Kaaba

I never thought I could make that climb. The side of the Kaaba is a straight height, a sheer wall, and the black, hanging cloth that gave me my only grip was frayed and loose with rotting. But at that moment had the Prophet asked me to fly, I might have become a famous miracle, 'Bilal the Flyer'.

When he asked me to go up, I knew, of course, why he needed me up. My presence on that roof, calling to prayer, would be a sign to mankind that this house built by Abraham had indeed been restored to the worship of God. My first call in Medina had, as the Prophet said, completed his Mosque; my call now would complete his cleansing of the Kaaba.

The responsibility was awesome. I was, in fact, climbing against the gods and had I fallen back the pagans would have seen in my broken body a reassertion of their gods. But, as I've said before, when the muezzin climbs to make the call it is the hope and raised faces of men that carry him up.

Sometimes hanging by my arms, kicking into the cloth to find a hold, my knees skinned, my breath in gasps, my heart a hammer, my ribs nearly wrenched from my backbone – I pulled, clawed, lifted myself up. The last yard was the longest. But I got to the top and rolled my body over onto the flat roof. I lay there out of sight of the world, and I remember wanting to stay that way, but the man who calls to prayer may not waste any of God's time on himself.

Below me all was silence. A multitude without a word. I stared up at the sky and it too seemed to be holding its breath; not a stir of air. Suddenly I was frightened. I understood where I was and what was expected of me.

I made the call. I made it well. I know I made it well because I heard it echo back, cry back, from the hill of Arafat. Every holy place replied.

I saw the Prophet sitting on his camel with his head bent and one hand laid upon the other. Only he was mounted. Closest to him stood the beautiful company of Ali, Abu Bakr, Omar and Abu Dharr, and around them and beyond them and on every side, the thousands, the tens of thousands, of women and men whose wars had ended in prayers.

Often at night I wake both in joy and frightened memory, remembering that day. Did it all happen as I say it did? Or am I back again, a slave squatting among slaves, grateful for the shade of a wall I imagined I climbed? Do I slip past memory into dream?

Old bones do not make a climber – and surely that time I had enough age upon me. Yet I have never been sure what age is. Mind and body are forever fighting that question and, even now, as I sit in the doorway, gazing out over the top of my stick into the setting sun, I ask myself – am I an old man who is young or a young man who is old?

History saw me climb. I did not dream it. My hope is that God saw me and I am already that far up, the height of the Kaaba, towards Heaven. If so, I am indeed Bilal the Flyer.

HISTORY PAGE SEVEN

Two years and two months after the Conquest of Mecca
Mohammad fell sick, probably with pneumonia, in
Medina. After an illness of ten days, on 8 June 632 he
died in the arms of Aisha, his youngest wife, the
daughter of Abu Bakr.
He was in his sixty-third year.

Bilal
tells of
Mohammad's
death

God took the soul of His last prophet kindly. He died in the afternoon on 8 June 632, in the midst of love, with the women weeping and the men hushed. They even say that when the Angel of Death visited him he asked politely if he was ready.

It is certain that all the prophets have not died easy deaths. Eli fell from a chair and broke his neck; Saul died by his own hand and his sons with him; Aaron died naked and shivering on the top of a mountain; the Man of God from Judah was eaten by a lion on the road; Solomon, for all his wisdom, loved women too dangerously and began to worship the goddess of Sidon, so God rent Israel from him and divided it into twelve parts; Moses was denied a tomb and his sister Miriam was struck by leprosy. But for Jesus men see different deaths. His believers insist he died in bloodshed, God's own flesh and blood, crucified among thieves; but we, who are also his followers, have quieter news. Christ died unpierced, a wanderer in a distant country, from where God took him up.

Though men may die in company, in wars, by infections, in the drowning of ships, every man's death is single to himself. No man may seek to understand another man's death. He can only relate its events, as I will now relate to you the events of the death of Mohammad, the Messenger of God, the last prophet.

It was a death neither sudden nor unsudden, neither violent nor easy, neither common nor uncommon – but it was the death of a man who was a prophet, a lamp lit in Heaven extinguished by the same Hand. Therefore it was unforeseen.

I woke him as usual and he came out as usual but more slowly. He complained of a headache and asked me to feel his forehead. I did and found him hot. I advised him to lie down again but he insisted on going with me to the Mosque. As we went he put his arm into mine and, because he seemed unsteady, I held him close. Suddenly, he paused: 'Do you remember, Bilal, the first time we met . . . we walked like this . . . but then it was I who was holding you up . . .'

He laughed and I laughed. 'It was twenty-two years ago,' I said.

'Yesterday, yesterday,' he replied.

That was our last happy time together. All that day and the next days I saw the fever gaining on him. But still he got up and, though his voice weakened and his hands trembled, he led the prayers.

On the fifth day, Aisha, her hair uncombed and her face distraught, opened the door. Behind her, I could hear Mohammad moaning and gasping for breath. She passed me a bucket and told me to bring cold water.

I ran, I ran, I ran past several wells to the deepest and coolest well of the oasis. I still hear the sound of the bucket splashing far down; water to fight his fires. But I had time only to bring the bucket to the door, for day was coming up and my responsibility was upon me. I knew that if the Prophet did not hear the morning call I would be putting a burden on his soul more than any pain in his body.

When I had finished, I went back to the door and again Aisha opened it. Now her hair was combed and braided, which was a sign for the good. 'He told me to tell you,' she said, 'that you never made a better call.'

I might have disagreed. I was often in truer pitch and, besides, that morning the air was heavier than usual and the palm trees were gobbling up the grace notes – if I did not fear God, after many a call I'd have given those Medina palm trees a whack of my stick. But let every muezzin know that his best call is not heard in the ear, which is only a machine, but in the heart, man's mind within. Therefore when the Prophet in his dying said that was my best call, then it was.

For two days he drifted between coma and waking and for two days I used my legs to run away from my mind. I never left his door except to run. I brought water from seven different wells hoping that one water might have a cure the other lacked. Aisha cooled his fever with the seven waters from seven bowls.

On the eighth morning there was a sudden change. He opened the door himself and came out, a white bandage tied round his head. With one hand on Ali's arm and the other on the arm of Fadl ibn Abbas, his nephew, he walked to the Mosque and prayed for the dead of Uhud.

But his step was slow and painful and I had to look away; even I, who am only a former slave, could see the visit of death on his face. So perhaps it is true what some men say and the Angel of Death did come and did go from him for three days.

That night, in the darkest hour of the night, he went into the cemetery and stood among the graves. Ali and I followed him, fearing he might fall, but he walked alone, firmly. He spoke into the blackness around him:

> 'Greetings to you, People of the Grave.
> Rejoice, for you are better off than men alive.
> The dawn that awakens you is more peaceful
> than the dawn that meets the living.'

When he came home he asked Aisha what money he had in the house and she didn't take long to count it. Seven dinars. 'Give them away tonight,' he said, 'for how can I meet God with this money still in my possession?'

Once more he came into the Mosque and this was the last time I saw him. He had only a few hours of life left but, strangely, the look of death had gone from him and I never saw him more beautiful. His face glowed with the joy of worship. He spoke gently, asking forgiveness of any he had wronged, warning them all to love the Koran, the revelation of God, a book of light and guidance. As he was helped up, he looked around at the living. 'I now go before you, but remember that you will follow me.'

What I tell you now I have only by report. In the pains of death, he lay in Aisha's arms. A man with toothpicks made of green wood came in and he asked for one. Aisha first chewed and softened the toothpick in her own mouth and then the Prophet took it and cleaned his teeth. As his strength sank she heard him say: 'O God, call me up on Doomsday with the poor.' Then other words . . . but they were unheard or lost or denied human hearing, for he was speaking to Heaven.

Suddenly the Messenger of God raised his head and gazed at the roof, seeing what only he saw. He spoke three words: 'The Highest Companion . . .'

By the witness of these three words it is supposed that in the moment of death Gabriel again came to him.

When we heard Aisha weeping we knew that Mohammad was dead.

Omar went in but his grief blinded him and he saw only a man sleeping. He did not see Mohammad dead. He came out raging, his fist in the air, shouting threats to anyone who talked of death. Several of us tried to hold him but he swept us off. Then he began to reason with his madness. 'Remember Moses,' he shouted. 'Moses went up to God on Mount Sinai. The Jews said he was dead. But what happened? What happened? After forty days he came back. After forty days Mohammad will come back, like Moses.' Poor noble Omar, he stood in the middle of the Mosque, his hair on end, turning this way and that, his grief charging against reality, like a madman throwing stones at the moon.

Abu Bakr also went in and looked down on Mohammad's face. There was no response and no doubt. He kissed him and drew a cloth over his face.

He came to the Mosque, this small, mild man, asking for silence, holding his hand above his head like a schoolboy in a schoolroom. But he spoke with the authority of all time: 'If there is anyone here who worships Mohammad, let him know that Mohammad is dead.' He paused to let this terrible truth take hold. 'But he who worships God, let him know that God is alive and does not die.'

Omar sank to the floor, his face in his hands, his huge body heaving in his crying.

I never called to prayer again. My legs could not carry me up and even when Ali and Abu Dharr helped me I broke down after the first words. My grief prevented me. I stood on the roof trying for words, finding one word, then half the next. I could not complete his name, 'Mohammad', and had to go back to the beginning four times, stammering, sobbing, failing again. Finally they took pity on me and helped me down.

Yet in my head five times a day I hear myself calling. I cup my ear and hear myself far away, in another city on another day, among other people. Sometimes I whisper it to my son when, like any child, he's played himself out and he's soundly sleeping.

After Mohammad's death, Abu Bakr was appointed Caliph, or Successor. The Successor had, of course, no succession as prophet. He managed the state and maintained the completed religion.

Abu Bakr ruled Islam with a gentle hand for two years then he, too, caught fever. As he was dying he asked for a pen and parchment and named Omar to succeed him.

Omar, they say, ruled Islam with his stick. But he was pious and humble. When he received the news of the conquest of Alexandria, a city of three hundred pleasure palaces, he was sitting under a tree sharing a handful of dates with his old slave. He came on foot to accept the surrender of Jerusalem, leading his camel because it was the old slave's turn to ride.

Bilal again appears only fleetingly. He went north to the army in Syria – it is said to seek martyrdom – and was present at the entry into Jerusalem. But it is not known that he fought in any battle.

Although grief silenced Bilal, he did make the call to prayer on two other occasions, several years apart. Once, 'that once only', by public petition and by the request of Omar, he made the call in Jerusalem. Then, again, when he came back to Medina to visit the grave of Mohammad, he was met by the grandchildren of the Prophet, Hasan and Husain, who begged him to make a last call. He felt he could not refuse. Although it was early morning, the streets were filled with weeping people.

Some unreliable reports make Bilal the Governor of Damascus. But while it is possible in every respect to see Bilal a governor – in concern, in the authority of his past, in love – it is almost impossible to see him a governor in office. He would have preferred to sit in a humble doorway.

The date of Bilal's death is uncertain. It was probably A.D. 644 – year 22 of the Hegira.

Bilal
in his
doorway

Life and the memory of it – that is an old man's triumph.

If any will remember me, let him remember me by my friends. Say to any who inquires about me: 'Bilal was his companion.' For I was one of that company who lived in the Perfect Time, the time the Messenger of God was alive. No one will ever know our shining days again, yet all may share their evidence.

Do not judge me because I was the first. My call might vary day to day and sometimes, perhaps by the will of God, the wind was a critic and threw the words back at me, or the morning damp rose to my throat, or the pigeons bothered me.

Let it be remembered, even in the sky, the Prophet called Bilal 'a man of Paradise'.

But few of us are left and those still with me will soon be going. It is not right to run forward to death, but it is right to look forward.

The living have the habit of thinking themselves better off than the dead. But they never ask themselves the question – do the dead agree with them? What did Mohammad mean that night in the graveyard when he called the dead fortunate?

The night was cold, I remember, the ground was hard and the People of the Grave neither stirred nor spoke. Each lay in his own pit. But were they the dead – or just the dry remains of a moisture once called man? For the body is only a river carrying the soul and it changes yard by yard, pool by pool, each body in its own flow, each body to its own final drought.

Yet I think I know what the Prophet meant. Once, when we were sitting in the Mosque – it was in the darkness before a thunderstorm, the clouds were coming in over Uhud and the hens, those clever weathercocks, were already running for cover – I heard him say: 'Men are asleep and when they die they waken!'

I regret no single day; not even the day I was whipped.

I am glad for children. Our children are as much our past as they are our future. A man finds his own father, finding him in himself, when he cares for his own son. It is a mystery of generation that although it is the old who teach the young, it is the young who improve the old.

I am glad of myself, my skin, my Africa, because in this dimension, I am.

I live now on my stick, my rounds are narrow, from this doorway to the Mosque, then home again. But I have more space than ever I had for I live in delighted memory of Mohammad.

Perhaps in the gardens of the blissful dead, I will walk again with Abu Dharr and hear him tell again that the evil of the world is property, that no one should possess more than he needs, that Mohammad had only two shirts, one for washing and one for wearing. I would hear again Abu Dharr argue the logic of the future – his eyes bright with thought – and the Prophet listening. For God sent Mohammad as a mercy to mankind and he was a prophet who loved to listen to men.

O God, grant that Abu Dharr be my sponsor in Paradise.

But meanwhile I'll chuckle at them a few more days here in Damascus and speak a little more in the old style.